Legacy Redeemed,

Legacy Redeemed,

The Second Son

AWARD-WINNING AUTHOR

C. S. ARNOLD

ReadersMagnet, LLC

Legacy Redeemed, The Second Son
Copyright © 2021 by C.S. Arnold

Published in the United States of America
ISBN Paperback: 978-1-955603-58-4
ISBN Hardback: 978-1-955603-59-1
ISBN eBook: 978-1-955603-57-7

All rights reserved. No part of this publication may be reproduced, stored in a retrieval system or transmitted in any way by any means, electronic, mechanical, photocopy, recording or otherwise without the prior permission of the author except as provided by USA copyright law.

The opinions expressed by the author are not necessarily those of ReadersMagnet, LLC.

ReadersMagnet, LLC
10620 Treena Street, Suite 230 | San Diego, California, 92131 USA
1.619.354.2643 | www.readersmagnet.com

Book design copyright © 2021 by ReadersMagnet, LLC. All rights reserved.
Cover design by Ericka Obando
Interior design by Mary Mae Romero

Dedication

To my husband, my best friend, who has supported me all the way through my writing efforts.

Also, by the author:

Novels

Dangerous Legacy, the Second Son – Given an "Editor's Choice' award by the publisher, iUniverse. Rated 4 of 4 by OnLineBookClub.org
Standing in My Shadow. March 2021

Children's Books:

The Patchwork Princess, Adventures of Ra-me, a Traveling Troubadour – Book 1
Won the Pinnacle Book Achievement Award for December 2019

Blaze the Dragon, Adventures of Ra-me, a Traveling Troubadour – Book 2
Won the Pinnacle Book Achievement Award for December 2019

Mudcat the Pirate, Adventures Ra-me, a Traveling Troubadour – Book 3
Won the Pinnacle Book Achievement Award for December 2019

Miscellaneous

Short, short stories in various faith-based papers
Other short stories

Characters traveling on the Baltic Queen from America to Poland
Stefan Zurowski
Sophia Zurowski
Konrad and Jan Zurowski (children)
Monica Milewski
Ishmael "Ish" Jacobson
Manke Jacobson (Ish's wife)
Dr Stanislas Janda (referred to as Stan, Stanislas, or Dr. Janda)
Captain Joyce, skipper of the *Baltic Queen*

Characters interacted with in Poland
Frederic Debrewski, estate overseer
Kasia Debrewski, Frederic's sister
Leah Jacobson, Nurse, and Ishmael "Ish" Jacobson's niece
David Jacobson: well-known resistance fighter throughout the Warsaw Ghetto, "Ish's" Jacobson's younger brother, and Leah's father
Sarah, rescued refugee
Jack MacKensie, Owner of Scottish Wool Concern, but filling in as temporary pastor in estate chapel
Mr. Wócjak, jeweler in Warsaw
Dr. Marcin Kowalski, new doctor for estate
Nurse Barbara Kowalski, doctor's wife
Pastor Angus Stewart, new Protestant pastor for estate chapel
Pastor's wife, Elsie and daughter, Skye
Family met in cabin on the way to Warsaw from *Domani z Camin*: Antoni, Lena, and Szymn Kaminski
Father Kowaski, Catholic priest who traveled with Jacobson from Danzig

Beginning

Jedwabne, Poland, July 10, 1941

Soviet invaders were in the town; then the Nazis came. Some locals stirred up the feeling that the Jewish population had been too welcoming to the Soviets when they invaded Jedwabne. Polish neighbors joined with the Nazi soldiers in the bloody massacre of the Jewish population. Few escaped.

Chapter 1

Two years later in an established Nazi camp not far from Jedwabne.

The naked night sky melted to earth giving Leah Jacobson the cover she needed to slip unnoticed from the military compound. Polish patriots were beginning to fight back. The noise from the surprise raid on the Nazi camp followed her into the surrounding wooded area. Cries from the wounded mingled with the sound of gunfire and the sulfur-y smell of burnt gunpowder hung in the still air.

"Leah?"

The voice came faintly through the night. She knew that voice: Bruno Stroop. She had heard it every day since he captured her in Jedwabne and brought her to the camp with him. Stroop had led his German troops in first; and when he left, he left the order for the Jews to be killed. She didn't know what had happened to her father, and she was sure he didn't know her fate.

She stood still. The voice calling her name reached her once again. There was a loud explosion and then all was silent. She felt the load lift. She felt free. But free to go where?

Leah only knew that tonight she must get as far away from the camp as possible. The Polish patriots would probably be crushed by the better-armed Germans. Then, reconnaissance patrols would round up those trying to escape. She had left at the first hint of the attack, so she did have a head start. The surrounding terrain was beginning to get lush and green, and some growth hid dangerous bogs that developed in poorly draining lake basins. She knew her progress would be slow as she avoided being stuck in the unforgiving mire, but her footsteps would be swallowed up by the sludge. Maybe she couldn't be followed easily.

Polish neighbors joined in with the invading Nazis to slaughter nearly the entire Jewish population in her hometown of Jedwabne. She knew of a few who had escaped, but she hadn't been so fortunate. A Nazi officer named Bruno Stroop was tall, muscular, and arrogant. He saw her and wanted her, claiming her as his share of the spoils of war. Her beauty was well-known in Jedwabne, and she had been a little vain. But her vanity disappeared as Stroop used her. At first, his attentions had been lustfully forced upon her, but her fighting spirit had caused him to look at her as more than just an object for his satisfaction. His professions of affection were harder to bear than his forcefulness had been. She hated his arrogance, his pride. She hated everything about him and what he stood for. If her life had been the only consideration, she might have ended it. But now a small life had begun within her.

When he thought that she might be carrying his child, he declared that she would return home with him. Her Nordic blonde beauty belied her Jewish heritage, but he assured her no one would dare question his choice. She had been planning her escape, and the attack on the camp provided the perfect opportunity. Bruno was the camp commander and was busy with his troops, leaving her in their quarters alone.

It was now or never. If she perished, she perished. Her child would die with her, but better to die than live the life Bruno Stroop had planned.

Domani z Camin. The name came to her. The estate of the Zurowski's wasn't too far, and the word at the camp was that it was now deserted. The Russians were there first, but they had moved further on when the Germans arrived. No sooner had the German troops been lodged there, than they abruptly abandoned the estate. It had been a mystery to Stroop and the other German officers. Rumor had it that the order came from a highly-placed source, so they followed the order and moved on.

She knew that it was north of Jedwabne, close to Wegorzewo, and if she could get there it would be a place to stay now that it was unoccupied. There she would rest from her journey and make plans. Perhaps there, she could think of her next move. She couldn't dare to hope that she would find assistance there.

Evening fog was drifting down through the trees, and Leah knew she would need to find a place to sleep during the night. One misstep could leave her to die in these swamps. Wolves were a danger, and bears and lynx also lurked at night. Snakes were her greatest fear. At the camp, she'd heard talk of the European viper as being extremely poisonous. Her shoes were sturdy but didn't come above her ankles. And there would be no way to see these snakes at night.

Suddenly, she dropped to the ground and kept still. She heard a noise. There it was again. But it came as a moan this time, soft and weak. Adjusting her focus to the area around her, she saw what looked like a pile of rags in a small ditch at the end of a clearing.

Slowly, she approached and saw the form of a child. The girl was unconscious but was beginning to waken. Her long, dark hair was matted and her bare arms and legs had been scratched by the thickets. She opened her eyes and stared at Leah.

"Help me," she whispered. Then she again lost consciousness.

Leah couldn't leave her, but it was going to be hard enough traveling alone without the responsibility of this girl. Even if she awakened, would she be strong enough to make the journey? And where did she come from? Someone might be looking for her, and Leah had to put as much distance between her and Bruno as she could. She knew that Bruno would be successful in putting down the camp rebellion, and his next order of business would be to find her. He would never stop looking for her now that she carried his child.

Leah made a dry bed of grass under a tree. For the night, she would hold the girl next to her for warmth and comfort with her one blanket wrapped around them both. She had given her a few sips of water which she swallowed even in her sleep. The child she held in her arms felt small, maybe not even ten years old. Leah had escaped with only the small amount of food and water she could secrete in her pack: barely enough for one person for a couple of days. She wouldn't think too far ahead. Tonight, they'd rest.

Leah prayed to a God she no longer believed existed, but it would be her only hope.

Morning dropped the warmth of the sun like a blanket over the sleeping forms of Leah and the girl in her arms. One arm had lost feeling, and she struggled to withdraw it from under the still-sleeping child.

"Oh, who are you?" The girl sat up straight, drawing back, her eyes wide.

"Don't be scared, my name's Leah, and I found you last night over by the stream. What's your name?"

"I'm Sarah," she whispered. Her eyes were still wide as she looked around.

"Where are your people, Sarah?" Leah asked, gently.

"Gone," she could barely whisper. "Soldiers came into our village and marched us all out. I don't know where we were going, but while I wasn't looking Mama pushed me down a hill. I hit my head, and that's all I remember. Why would she do that?"

She started to cry. "She left me. Will the soldiers come looking for me?"

"I doubt it, Sarah. When you hit your head, you looked hurt and they wouldn't have stopped for you. Your mama did that to save you, Sarah. People from the villages are being taken to camps to become slaves for their captors. Your momma wanted you to escape," Leah explained. "She knew you'd be brave and find help." *She'd heard jokes at the camp about victims they'd left. There was no use the girl knowing that her folks were probably being marched to a concentration camp for execution. She would realize soon enough that she'd never see them again.*

"You found me?" Sarah asked.

"Yes, I found you, and we'll be ok." Maybe if she could get Sarah to believe it, she would believe it too.

"Where are we going?" asked Sarah. She had attached her future to Leah's. "Where are your people?"

"My home was in Jedwabne before I was taken to the camp. I'm trying to get to Domani z Camin because I've heard there aren't any soldiers there." The words were taking on determination as Leah spoke them aloud to Sarah.

"Where are your mama and poppa? Won't they be looking for you?" Sarah wondered.

"No, my mama died when I was born, and my poppa may have been taken away by soldiers." *Leah could still remember the faint screams she had heard from a distance as her neighbors attacked and killed the Jews that had once been friends. Hatred had boiled over, annihilating the entire village. She'd not seen her father since; she just hoped that he'd gotten away. Bruno assured her that he saw her father run into the woods and didn't see anyone giving chase. But why would she trust him?*

"We have to keep in the shade of the trees, out of the water, and on the lookout for snakes and strangers," said Leah.

Sarah laughed and Leah couldn't help but join her. Maybe the trip would be better with two.

"I'm eight years old, you know, and I'm quite grown up," said Sarah emphatically. "My head hurts, but I think that's just a good sign that I'm alive."

"Right you are, kid, right you are," Leah was smiling.

They shared some dried fruit and water, after which Leah refilled her canteen from the creek, and they began their trip north. The child was limping slightly.

Chapter 2

The limousine driver pulled under the porte-cochere in front of the mansion. He exited the driver's seat, walked briskly around to the other side, opened the door, and stepped back as his passenger got out of the vehicle. Vincent Ludlow watched as the chauffeur carefully deposited his Mark Cross luggage at the massive entrance doors, returned to the vehicle, and drove it around the main house where he would park it in the wide garage housing the other vehicles belonging to the estate. Ludlow had been here many times for both business and pleasure, and he was familiar with Forest House and the people who kept it running smoothly. He knew the chauffeur's quarters were above the garage, and this driver, along with much of the estate's staff had been here for many years. Most of them came with Jósef Zurowski when he'd established his residence here in Forest House in Dark Forest, Minnesota.

Vincent Ludlow was here this day to bring news, and whether the news was good or bad depended on each individual whom it impacted. It had been too confidential not to deliver in person; so Jósef had sent his private plane to New York so the documents could be delivered quickly. He had his limousine waiting at the airport.

Ludlow held his briefcase to his chest, stepped up to the door, and rang a bell which he knew would be heard only in the required part of the house.

The butler opened the door quickly. "Good afternoon, Mr. Ludlow. Did you have a comfortable journey?" asked Antek.

"It was good, thank you, Antek. Jósef Zurowski knows how to plan a trip." The two men chuckled together.

"That he does, sir. I'll announce you," said Antek. He took the Brooks Brothers topcoat and the fedora the visitor handed him. "Mr. Zurowski is in the library if you'll follow me."

Vincent Ludlow had been the Zurowski's attorney since Jósef immigrated to America and needed his first contract executed. Ludlow owed his own success to this client. The business they'd be discussing now would be the riskiest venture to date.

Antek opened the library door and stepped in.

"Mr. Ludlow is here, sir," he announced. Then he turned and left, closing the door silently behind him.

Jósef stood to greet Vincent, and the two shook hands. "Glad you're here, Vincent. So much to do now that we have word that it's a go." He sat back down as though pushed down by the enormity of the coming task.

"Yes," agreed Vincent.

"But it's going to be at least two hours before dinner, so let me ring for Antek to show you to your room, so you can get a little rest. The discussion can wait until after dinner; it may be a long night," said Jósef. He stood and pulled the bellrope.

"Thank you," said Vincent. "I'm still working on a list of questions that only could be answered in person."

"Good," Jósef offered. "Manka has fresh szarlotka for lunch and coffee."

"Ah, yes, Manka's Polish apple pie. I was in too much of a rush to eat lunch," said Vincent.

Antek knocked softly on the door and entered.

"Antek, please take Mr. Ludlow to his room and have Manka take him a piece of szarlotka and a carafe of coffee," Jósef instructed.

Briefcase in hand, Ludlow followed Antek from the room.

Marie had ordered a beautiful dining table to be set. Crystal and silver gleamed under the light from the chandelier above. Snowy white napkins were a background for the Z's embroidered in silver thread. Marie loved entertaining, but Jósef never invited business associates into his private life. For Vincent Ludlow, an old friend as well as their attorney, he made an exception.

Jósef sat at the head of the table, Marie on his right. Stefan sat at the other end of the table with Sophia on his right. Mrs. Mileski sat next to Sophia and Vincent Ludlow sat next to Marie. Jósef had insisted that Ish and Manka also be at the table.

As was the new custom since Stefan came to live at Forest House, he said the blessing over the food before they ate. A quiet chorus of 'amens' followed Stefan's benediction.

The steaming heat was as welcome as the flavor of the rich borscht with cream. They could take comfort from the warmth of the soup against the chill of the upcoming discussion. The soup things were cleared away and the *pike au gratin* was served generously buttered and toasted brown. Jósef was proud of the fish caught from their own lakes. The *śćąhąb więpżówy* was done to perfection. And with this pork loin, baked sauerkraut and yellow peas. The freshly churned butter was offered to spread on the *chlęb żytni*. The aroma of the caraway seeds added another layer of flavor to this rye bread.

"Manka, this is the best cheesecake I've ever eaten," said Vincent. Manka lowered her head to hide her blush.

"We do eat well," Jósef added, smiling at Manka's embarrassment.

The diners lingered over the sernik and coffee, putting off the discussion that was to come.

"Alright. Dinner is over, let's all go to the library, it's time to hear what Vincent has come to tell us." Jósef's clipped speech left no room for argument as he led the way.

"No doubt you all remember the situation we had here at Forest House a few years ago when the Nazi Art Committee attempted to steal the Zurowski Jeweled Crucifix," Jósef began, "and now we've heard from them once again. Stefan and I have kept this a secret for your safety, but now you need to know."

"Yes," said Ish, "it was a dangerous situation orchestrated by an undercover SS officer by the name of Bruno Krump, masquerading as Father Vladek. As I recall, he had murdered Father Vladek before the priest could leave Danzig to take up his new parish here in Dark Forest. Krump assumed the priest's identity and sailed here on the *Baltic Queen*."

"Yes, that's right," Stefan nodded, then continued. "Because of Uncle Jósef's vital contributions to the war effort, our government is allowing us to consider this latest request in the negotiations. If we accept their terms, it could affect you all."

"Before we go any further in our discussion," Jósef interrupted, studying his nephew's face, "are you quite sure of your decision, Stefan?"

"I have no second thoughts, Uncle Jósef. Domani z Camin with its land must be saved, saved for now and the future; I'll take the risk. The question remains: does anyone of you want to go?"

"Make this plainer, Jósef," demanded Marie. "Go where? Do what?"

"I'm sorry, my dear," said Jósef, realizing she was completely confused. He explained further: "The Nazi command in Poland proposes to return Domani z Camin to Zurowski control in exchange for the jeweled crucifix. All German soldiers have been routed off the estate and a 'kill' order is posted at its gate."

Stefan picks up the narrative: "I will travel to Poland aboard the *Baltic Queen* and be escorted by German forces to a meeting in Warsaw with a trusted Hitler aide. There, I will exchange the crucifix for signed papers leaving the estate in our hands."

The group was silent. Each asking the same question within: *Can we trust these terms? These people?*

Vincent Ludlow joined the conversation. "The Nazi relations office put a cash offer on the table a year after the NAC withdrew from Dark Forest. The offer amounted to a great deal of money."

"We declined their offer," said Jósef, "and responded back with an offer of our own. Why," he asked Vincent, "do you think they've waited so long to respond to our proposal?"

"I wish I knew," Vincent answered. "Maybe they'd been trying to have their cake and eat it, too. Get the crucifix and keep the estate. Maybe they thought it would make them look weak to have you back in charge of Domani z Camin. Appearance means a lot to the Germans. Who knows what they are thinking?"

"We've worked hard in the war effort here on our end to help where we could," said Stefan "and now here's our chance to reclaim our Polish land. Perhaps if Domani z Camin is restored, it can provide some safety for those who've had to be in hiding."

Vincent Ludlow opened his briefcase and pulled out the latest document from the NAC. "There doesn't appear to be any hidden agenda, but it is a considerable risk when we consider with whom we're dealing. This document states: 'as per your request the Zurowski lands are now abandoned without further damage. The castle is no longer occupied by military troops, and orders have gone down from the highest German authority that it is off-limits to German and/or Russian soldiers on penalty of immediate death'."

"So, now," said Stefan, "all that remains is for me to take the Zurowski Jeweled Crucifix to the Nazi Art Committee. That's the last step. It seems the NAC attributes extrinsic merit to this religious artifact as much as its monetary value. Hitler is evermore obsessed now with things of the occult, frantically searching and drawing them around him. He's either convinced his Art Committee of this fact, or they have no alternative but to accept his beliefs. The crucifix has prospered the Zurowskis since it was gifted to them by a priest of a most Holy Order, but I'm not sure if this prosperity can be expected to follow the ownership of the crucifix. I guess such arrogance as we're dealing with here wouldn't consider such a possibility," concluded Stefan.

"I've listed a couple of reasons why these negotiations have moved forward," said Ludlow. He pulled another sheet of paper from his briefcase. "After the fall of France, Adolph Hitler hoped the British government would accept his offer to end the war. Which of course, we know they refused."

"Exactly," agreed Ish, "and Hitler reluctantly considered invasion only as a last resort. I believe their planned attack on the British Isle's code name was Operation Sea Lion."

Ludlow resumed reading from his list: "In the Battle of Britain, the Luftwaffe sustained crippling losses and the Royal Air Force continued bombardment with no sign of stopping. I think the figure was two German planes lost to every one of the RAF. The British fought in the air and endured underground. The result was that Operation Sea Lion was called off. That was in the fall of 1940."

"Sophia and I were in South America directing the opening of another copper mine during that fall and the following spring, and by the time we got the news it was stale." Stefan winked at Sophia. That business trip had doubled as their honeymoon.

"Hitler may have begun to feel his power slipping at this point since he wouldn't be able to destroy the Allied Forces landing sites along the Channel and further coastal positions," said Jósef. "But he continued bombarding ports and industrial sites to demoralize them."

"For whatever reason, we now have the possibility of reclaiming the Polish Zurowski Estate with the responsibilities we owe to those families who have been living there for generations," Stefan's shoulders lifted, ready to accept his legacy.

"This operation is secret," admonished Jósef, "and the fewer people who know of our plans, the safer we all will be. No one else is to be told unless Stefan and I agree that it's necessary."

"I did tell Monica while I was in New York," said Ludlow. "But she's sworn to secrecy, and she is part of this family."

"I hope she's discrete for her own sake," Stefan wasn't happy with this news.

"So, now we make plans for your trip to Poland. You'll have many hidden friends among the underground patriots, but there's still the dangerous journey from here to there. U-boats and hidden mines will be the biggest threats," Jósef warned. "I've read in the newspapers that Hitler has offered a $1,000,000 reward to any U-Boat skipper and crew that would sink the *Queen Mary* while carrying troops. The German 'wolfpacks' can contain up to ten submarines that would attack an unsuspecting ship at night. Their land blitzes have worked so well, I guess they've taken the strategy underwater."

Still puzzled, Marie asked, "But how does this affect the others in this room?"

"There may be some in this room who want to go with Stefan," Jósef looked around as he spoke. "Vincent will need time to prepare new passports or renew old ones. The list of those going will have to be given to the State Department who is arranging an open-ended approval to stay in Poland."

"I'm going." It was Ish Jacobson. "Perhaps I can find my brother David."

"Not without me," Manka said, taking his hand.

"We'll go as a family," interrupted Sophia with an uncharacteristic bite to her words. "You do remember 'whither thou goest I will go; and where thou lodgest…'?"

Stefan turned his head quickly to Sophia, and she held his eyes.

"It'll be a culture shock that you can't prepare yourselves for," said Stefan, his countenance darkening as his thoughts went back. "I saw landscapes that should've been familiar twisted beyond recognition, orphaned children begging in the streets but terrified to make human contact. You'll see things that will tear your heart out. The horror I saw behind the Russian soldiers as they left Domani z Camin will be forever with me. The crippling pain from those images has eased, but their shadows will darken my soul forever. The loss of my family in Poland is for always," Stefan paused, looking around, "but my new family here is my consolation."

Sophia had been listening with her heart. She walked to Stefan and he pulled her into his arms.

"But we're talking about Domani z Camin, its surviving people, and all it stands for, Stefan," said Ish. "I must go back." He looked around as the others nodded their assents.

"Then, we'll have to pray for safety," Stefan said. His faith wasn't shared by his Uncle, and he didn't know about the others; but Stefan's belief stood firm. He looked around his circle of family and friends and smiled. "And we'll thank God for the new sonar that we've ordered installed on the *Baltic Queen!*"

Chapter 3

Stefan Zurowski looked over the fields at Forest House. The temperate weather this year had allowed the farmhands to complete spring planting early, and tiny shoots of growth were reaching for the sun. The pastures were overflowing with new life. Newborn calves frolicked and kicked as they ran in the open fields. Colts awkwardly gamboled in the paddocks as their dams grazed nearby. The farm was in good order, and it was a convenient time to leave things in the hands of others. It was time to move forward.

Even in the face of war in Europe, he was blessed. He had a loving wife and two sons. When he fled to America from his home in Poland, he had no idea that he could become so immersed in life here in Minnesota. But Minnesota boasted many lakes as did his home in the Masurian Lake District of Poland. His new relatives welcomed him, and the four years had passed quickly. His Uncle Jósef had made him his sole heir, sharing many of his responsibilities, expanding Stefan's knowledge of his vast empire and grooming him to take the lead when the time came.

Count Zurowski had hated his son even to his dying breath. Stefan's mother had died giving him life, and his father blamed the child and his accusation never wavered. But as bitter as it was, it was in the past.

Jósef and Stefan had worked here in America together to aid the Polish underground as it emerged. Many of the guns and ammunition they had furnished made their way through the sewers into the Warsaw Ghetto to be used by those trying to provide some form of protection against the guards. The firepower gave their escape plans more of a chance of success. But mostly, they sent food and clothing: the basic essentials withheld by their captors.

Ships from New York to Danzig ghosted in under cover of darkness, offloaded their goods, and disappeared through the foggy dawn. Now it was time to be a human presence in this war-torn country. Stefan knew if he could get safely to Domani z Camin and could find his tenants, he had the means to lift the burdens from their shoulders and reclaim the Zurowski land.

He had written to Frederic, his father's steward, and he had received an answer. The house in Danzig where he and his sister Kasia lived had been destroyed, but they had escaped unharmed. Stefan wrote back telling Frederic where to meet him. He would have to inform him of a time when the plans were settled. Frederic and Kasia could now make their home permanently at Domani z Camin.

Stefan hoped that many would experience Domani z Camin as a sanctuary. They'd all work together to make it so. Ish Jacobson wanted to accompany him, and Stefan knew he would be invaluable. Uncle Jósef had depended on the younger man ever since coming to America, and Ish knew Poland and its people. Stefan knew that there was more to Ish than he'd first believed. He loved to be involved in the landscaping at Forest House and the gardens, but there were depths to the man that Stefan expected to learn as they traveled together.

Chapter 4

"We'll be sending different cargo this trip," said Jósef. "In case the *Baltic Queen* is boarded, we won't be able to send any military aid. This should protect the personnel that will be going. I've ordered a new tractor on which a shovel attachment can be secured. Ordered two shovels, also. And, of course, the bulldozer. The lands have been torn up from the bombing. The sooner a runway can be built, the more quickly our planes can bring in supplies," said Jósef.

"Uncle, when do you think this equipment will be ready?" asked Stefan.

"Delivery to the New York harbor has been promised in thirty days; I only wish I were going with you," said Jósef.

"It looks like Dr. Janda's son is going with us," Stefan said. "His father insists a doctor will be needed there more than a second doctor here in Dark Forest. Stanislas will put off taking over his father's practice for a while, and he is now preparing a list of medical supplies and equipment."

"That's a relief to me. I'm concerned with the possibility of our people becoming sick with the conditions that they'll encounter. Have they all been inoculated?" asked Jósef.

"Stanislas is getting the serums ready and will give the injections as soon as he receives the medicine," said Stefan. "I'm still fighting with the women who say they're going with us."

Jósef chuckled. "Well, good luck with that."

"Sophia says that she won't be left. And she insists that traveling with our children will make us look less intimidating. Of course, Manka is determined to go along to help care for the children. But I think she doesn't want Ish to go without her," said Stefan.

"Aw, yes, a romance of long-standing," said Jósef.

"I guess you'll lose your cook for a while," Stefan teased.

"She's sure a fine cook, but Ish is desperate to find his brother, David. He was from Jedwabne, and the news from there in 1941 was that nearly all had perished. He is hoping that somehow his brother had escaped. And, he had a niece there. He said her name is Leah. That massacre on Jedwabne happened two years after you left.

The next thirty days were a whirlwind of activity, but things progressed on time. Only a few people would be going, because they wanted to hire as many workers as possible from among the locals when they reached Poland. Dr. Stanislas Janda had administered all the vaccinations and procured the needed medical supplies. Stefan watched Sophia pack all their clothes and those needed for three-year-old Konrad and one-year-old Jan who was named in memory of Sophia's twin brother. She'd said Jan could wear Konrad's hand-me-downs, but she'd packed larger, new clothes to outfit Konrad as he grew.

There had been a simple wedding for Ish Jacobson and Manka before they left, adding a joyous celebration to the group with nearly all the population of Dark Forest offering congratulations to their long-time friends.

Ish helped Manka pack non-perishable food and the utensils needed for preparation. He also gathered up hand tools that he knew might not be available and a variety of seeds to be planted.

Reports were that the castle at Domani z Camin had been plundered before it was abandoned, but perhaps the fields could be planted soon.

They spent many hours going over their lists. Their boxes would be stowed in the back of two canvas-covered trucks. Benches with padded seats and backrests were placed in the back of the third truck where the travelers would ride on the trip from Danzig to Domani z Camin. Replacement tires and parts for the trucks would also make the trip. The ship would be valuable cargo for any raider on the sea, but Captain Joyce had safely sailed the *Baltic Queen* from America to Poland for three trips. As far as onlookers were concerned, this was a private passenger ship. But a state-of-the-art defense system had been installed, and the crew onboard were well-trained in its operation.

Captain Joyce's first trip carried Stefan from Danzig to New York where Stefan then journeyed to Dark Forest, Minnesota. Stefan had been quarantined by the plague in sickbay for the entire trip. Two other clandestine voyages had carried aid to the suffering population as well as items considered contraband for the underground freedom fighters. It became unsafe to try again as the German occupation escalated.

Safety was still a factor, but the fear of not making a successful trip had to be suppressed. Personal lives would be on the line, but the past, present, and future of Domani z Camin depended upon this deal with the devil. This side play acting out on its small stage within the larger world theater was on track to be a winner. But one would have to wait to read the reviews.

Chapter 5

"I'm back! I'm home," the voice called out gaily. The taxi driver deposited a large number of bags in the entryway and headed back to his van.

"Monica, what a surprise," Aunt Marie stood, nearly speechless. "What are you doing back. Has New York lost it's luster?"

"Yes, I've used it up! Been to all the hot spots, bought all the latest fashions, eaten at all the fabulous restaurants, and tolerated all the fortune hunters. Quite an experience. Didn't think it would ever happen, but I missed Forest House and all of you," she said. Her voice had echoed through the house, bringing other family members to the entrance.

"Well, welcome back, dear," said her Aunt Marie.

"And who is this handsome fella?" Monica stooped to kneel before Konrad.

"I'm Konrad," he had a slight lisp.

"Ah, I see. Well, I'm your Aunt Monica," she shook his hand.

"Aunt Monkey? I'm free." He held up three small fingers.

"Well, Aunt Monkey will do," she said. "You're three! Have I been gone that long? So much has happened, I see. And this must be baby Jan." She held out her arms for the baby that Monica held.

"Monica, it's good to see you," Sophia stepped forward, handing the baby to her cousin.

"You, too, cuz. Glad to be back. Where are all the menfolk?" she asked.

"Stefan, Uncle Jósef, Ish, and a couple more are getting ready for the trip to Poland," explained Sophia.

"Yes, that's why I've returned now. Vincent Ludlow told me of the family plans. I'm part of the family, and I want to go, too."

"Monica, are you sure?" her aunt Marie asked. "It's not a lark; it's a dangerous trip."

"Aunt Marie, I've read all the papers. I know what's been going on, and I *need* to go," her eyes flashed determination.

'Yeah! Aunt Monkey, will go with us," shouted Konrad, clapping his small hands together.

"At least I have one fan," Monica said. "Sophia, I can help with the boys. I find that I'm quite good with children. I even volunteered at a daycare in New York while the mothers worked in a factory. I'm not totally useless. I didn't like being spit on by the babies, but I found I could get used to that. I even stopped wearing haute couture on my workdays. And I wore sensible shoes." Her laughter faded as she looked at the faces turned to her.

"My dear, how thoughtful," said Mrs. Milewski, her grandmother. "You can take all the hats and mittens I've knitted and give them to the children. Their hands will be so cold this winter."

"Please, don't make me beg?" Monica looked around at her astonished relatives. "I need to be a part of this," her eyes glistened with unshed tears.

"Monica, it's ok with me, but it's not my decision. Stefan will be the one to give his permission," said Sophia. "I'll be happy for you to help with the boys."

"Uncle Jósef won't be going?" she asked.

"No, dear," said her Aunt Marie. "There'll be even more for him to do here with Stefan and Ish gone. And Manka will be going, too."

"And Vincent said Stanislas will be going as the medical person," Monica said, "doctor, I mean." Her hands rubbed together nervously.

"You have my vote, Monica," agreed Sophia. "It'll be dangerous for the boys and me to go, but I won't have our family separated. I finally convinced Stefan to let us go with him."

"Put in a good word for me, Sophia," said Monica.

"If you need one," Sophia laughed. "But you can be pretty convincing on your own."

"My dear, this is good. You've been a butterfly too long. You need to be a worker bee." Her grandmother seemed to see the subject as settled.

"Let's prepare for dinner, and we will talk it over there," said Marie. "Manka said dinner will be ready at 6 o'clock as usual and the men will be back."

The family sat around the table. Uncle Jósef sat at the end with Marie on his right and Monica on his left. Stefan sat at the other end with Sophia at his right. Stanislas and Ish sat on either side. Manka would sit beside Ish, letting their kitchen maid serve.

Manka had prepared galumpkis. The cabbage leaves were a brilliant green and the mixture of meat, spices, and rice gave off the most tantalizing aroma. These cabbage rolls were baked in a tomato sauce which added flavor as well as color. The galumpkis were paired with kopytka. The potatoes in her dumplings cooked to perfection.

"Manka, I ate in a Polish restaurant in New York and ordered galumpkis," said Monica. "These are way better than what they served. I've missed your cooking," taking another cabbage roll onto her plate.

"You are too thin. Eat. Eat more," urged Manka. "If you're too thin, you'll get sick."

The szarloyka was served with coffee. This Polish apple pie had almonds and raisins with a crumble on top.

"And this szarloyka is not your all-American apple pie," said Monica as she lifted another forkful.

"So, Monica," began Uncle Jósef, "you want to go to Poland with the family?"

"Yes, Uncle, I do," she answered.

"You know you won't get food like this, don't you? Times there are hard and many barely have enough to keep them alive. Some have no food at all and no shelter," he continued.

"I know it won't be easy and that it's dangerous, but I think it's time I became a little more useful," she said.

"Doing what?" interrupted Stefan, sharply.

"Oh, I don't know… teach ladies how to dress, maybe give make-up tips, reveal the latest hairstyles…you know, things like that." She wasn't going to let Stefan beat her down.

"Now, Stefan, maybe Monica will be an asset. Konrad hasn't let his 'Aunt Monkey' out of his sight since she came. Sophia will be able to use the help since the children will have to be watched constantly. There will be all kinds of harm that could come to them, seen and unseen," said Jósef.

"And she can distribute the hats and mittens I've knitted for the children," added Mrs. Milewski, again.

"Goodness knows you've knitted enough hats and mittens over the last three years," Marie said, gently. "How many boxes have we packed already?"

"Ten," she answered proudly. "Large ones."

"Stefan, I will need extra help while you're busy," said Sophia.

"I don't mean to be stubborn, Monica, but you can't jump in a taxi and run back home. We may be there two years, depending on how much we can accomplish with the war going on around us," reasoned Stefan. "But I can see that I'm outnumbered."

"Is that a 'yes' then?" she asked.

"I think I hear a 'yes'," Uncle Jósef agreed.

"I guess that's settled, then, Monica," Stefan said. "You're going, and I hope we're all not sorry."

"Oh, pooh, Stefan. You worry too much," said Monica.

"Stefan, I can give her the necessary inoculations today," said Stanislas. "There's still time before we leave."

"I bet you'll enjoy that," said Monica. "You're sadistic."

"Does this discourage your trip?" asked Stanislas.

"Not on your life, doctor. I'm going."

Dinner was over and they all prepared to go their separate ways.

"Sophia, will you tell me what I need to pack?" asked Monica.

"Sure. I have the list that Kasia sent to Manka for us," said Sophia.

"Good," she said, adding, "I hope I don't get seasick."

When Sophia and Monica had left the room, Stefan groaned. "She doesn't know what lies ahead. This may damage her psychologically. She could have a breakdown."

"Give her some credit, Stefan," said Jósef, "she's tougher than you might think."

After the bombshell that Monica had dropped, the household quickly settled back into the plans for their imminent departure. Now they were in New York, and it was two days before departure on April 12, 1944. When Monica had gone to live in New York, Jósef had instructed Vincent Ludlow to purchase her an apartment. It was large enough for Stefan, Sophia, the boys, Ish, Manka, Monica, and Stanislas. Her staff had been retained for another month, so it went smoothly. Jósef and Marie spent the night in the home of Vincent Ludlow. It seemed a family bonding was occurring; and, hopefully, it was a bond that would hold tight for what was to come.

The next day the men went to the *Baltic Queen* to inventory the complete list of items on the ship. All was accounted for and battened down. The living quarters for the passengers had been prepared for comfort and safety, but it wouldn't prepare them for the hardships awaiting when they landed. The clothes they wore on ship would be left there. When they disembarked, they would be dressed to blend in with those milling in the streets.

Monica had made salon appointments with her hairdresser for them and insisted they go on a window-shopping trip after they'd finished. "It will be our last foray into the land of silks, cashmere, and satin," she insisted. And the other women couldn't help but laugh with her. Perhaps, they did need this release. Monica bought an armful of long, hi-fashion scarves. "Kasia's list said headscarves," she justified as she took her purchases from the clerk, "and I didn't own one headscarf."

"Sounds like a swell idea," agreed Manka. "Let's all get one."

"My treat," said Monica. "Let's pick out your colors! Green for Sophia, I think, with her auburn hair, and bright blue to match Manka's eyes. Aunt Maria, I think white for you."

Konrad and Jan bounced up and down as the shoppers walked into the apartment. The babysitter was smiling at the two boys. She was the niece of one of Monica's New York friends, so she came highly recommended. The boys had been bathed and wore their pj's, awaiting their promised surprises. Konrad was delighted with his Lego blocks, and Jan chewed happily on the ear of his new bear. Sophia and Monica fed the boys their supper, and Konrad insisted his 'Aunt Monkey' tell them a bedtime story.

The boys snuggled up with Sophia as Monica read about Winnie the Pooh. The story outlasted the boys, so Sophia covered them gently, turned out their light, and she and Monica left the room. The babysitter would stay while they went out to dinner, but the boys usually slept through the night without waking.

The women had returned to the apartment before the men got back. They showered, dressed, and lounged in the large living area by the window that looked out over the city where the lights were just beginning to make themselves known in the twilight. They looked like ladies of leisure and high fashion instead of innocents on the brink of entering a shattered country. But Vincent Ludlow had made a dinner reservation for them at Delmonico's, and they had to dress for that occasion.

The men had returned from the harbor in a somber mood. They had watched the *Queen Mary*'s embarkation from New York to disembark in Gourock, Scotland. The troops on board were said to number nearly 12,000 plus at least 1,000 crew. Fighting men on the way to bring freedom and relief to those under the thumb of Nazi Germany. They had waited on the dock silently until the *Queen Mary* had sailed through the narrows, the three towering smokestacks of the luxury liner disappearing over the horizon, the tugboats returned to the harbor.

Their lawyer, Vincent Ludlow, had completed all the necessary paperwork and had met them in New York when they arrived. He'd done a currency exchange for Polish zloty. He knew Stefan had devised several different ways to travel safely with a great deal of cash which would be required for this trip. He also knew that

Stefan planned to give each person with him money in case they were ever separated on the way to Domani z Camin. His sources said the Central Bank of Poland would be reestablished by next year, and then additional funds could be transferred.

All was in order, and Uncle Jósef and Aunt Marie accompanied the others to the harbor to see them board the ship. The *Queen Mary* had left, and the largest ship remaining was the *Baltic Queen*. A few curious onlookers strolled the dock, waiting to see if travelers were coming or going.

His chest tightened and tears blurred his vision as Jósef watched his family walk up the gangplank. Stefan, Sophia, Ish, Manka, Stanislas, and Monica boarded the *Baltic Queen*. Konrad held tightly to his 'Aunt Monkey's' hand, Stefan carried Jan. *Would he see them again, Jósef wondered?*

The real Zurowski treasure was its people: Stefan Zurowski's legacy defined. Jósef would go back to Dark Forest, Minnesota, picking up the reins again to keep the home front prospering, but alone as before, without Stefan. His shoulders slumped at this burdensome future. He couldn't entertain the thought that he would never again have his family back around him at Forest House. They watched the tugs safely guide the ship through the narrow waterway, and when the *Baltic Queen* was lost to view over the horizon, Jósef took Marie's arm and led her to their waiting limousine.

Chapter 6

In September of 1939, Stefan had spent his crossing on the *Baltic Queen* from Danzig to New York in sickbay. He'd probably contracted the plague in Warsaw as he journeyed to meet Frederic, and his survival was due to the excellent care of the doctor on board the ship who'd cared for other plague victims.

He remembered nothing of the first trip, and he was eager to explore the ship. The first week Captain Joyce proudly conducted a tour every day after lunch. Not as large as the *Queen Mary*, but the *Baltic Queen* was every bit as opulent. Each day was a new adventure. Multi-storied, the ship held many attractions. Grand staircases with gleaming, wooden banisters framed the wide flights of steps that led from some decks to others. The brasses were polished to a high luster. The theatre was state-of-the-art with plush seats, deep, thick carpets, and other acoustical features. Movies for the children had been added to the viewing choices. A room was set aside as a safe place for the boys to run and play.

The so-called Captain's Pool was at the disposal of the travelers who liked swimming. A shallow end had been constructed for the benefit of the two young boys. A second pool in another area was available for the crew.

The library held classics as well as the latest publications. Comfortable chairs with ottomans were strategically placed under reading lights. Writing desks were available with stationery embossed with the name of the *Baltic Queen* in gold letters.

The men were fascinated with the wirelesstelegraphy equipment installed on board. It allowed for constant communication with both Europe and America by telegraph, radio, telephone, and broadcast radio during their Atlantic crossing. The transmitting room was an unmanned equipment room. The receiving room was a couple of hundred feet forward of the transmitting room on the Sun Deck. Operator positions were arranged at a table: a telegraph typewriter and a Morse key at each operator position. There were separate work areas for the junior and senior radio officers. Several independent aerials were installed on the *Baltic Queen*. Uncle Jósef could be kept abreast of their sea voyage, and it would set his mind at ease.

All in all, the opulence of the ship along with the cuisine at the Captain's table did nothing to prepare them for arriving at their destination. It was only when they visited the cargo holds that they were reminded of the seriousness of their endeavor. The canvas-covered trucks, the tractor, and the bulldozer made their own silent declarations loud and clear.

Land had long since disappeared from view, and no other vessels had been seen. Sharks abounded in this choppy Atlantic. Stefan stood with the Captain early on the morning of the tenth day watching the red-gold sun arise from the eastern horizon.

"Captain, why do you think we've not seen any ships?" asked Stefan.

"I plotted our course to stay out of the main shipping lanes, but I'm certain we'll see a merchant ship soon," said Captain Joyce. "Our sonar has indicated a presence."

"A merchant ship will be delivering supplies to ports?" asked Stefan. "Is she in any danger?"

"She'd be a sitting duck alone, but they usually travel with escorts for protection," the Captain paused, "and some will have an aircraft escort."

Feet pounded as a crewman ran across the deck to the Captain. "Sir, we've intercepted a message."

"What is it?" asked the Captain.

The Senior Communications Officer handed a typed communique to the Captain and glanced at Stefan.

"You can speak in front of this man," the Captain said.

"Yes, sir," the sailor said. "The message wasn't in code, and we only had to translate it from the German.

The Captain's brow furrowed as he read the message. "The additional experimental communications equipment that your uncle ordered installed on the *Baltic Queen* is unbelievable. It's like we've been bounced a copy of a message sent from a U-boat to German Naval Command reporting the sighting of a lone merchant ship."

"One merchant ship with no protection?" asked Stefan. "The captain must have felt a degree of safety traveling out of the main sea lanes."

"Mariners are in danger as soon as land is out of sight, but to sail alone without an escort is suicide. Sharks aren't the only dangers deep in the Atlantic." The Captain continued to read the message. "It further says: '*Need no assistance. Will track this single ship today. Attack tonight*'."

Stefan thought of their own two escort ships, and he had occasionally spotted their aircraft escort. "Is there anything we can do?" asked Stefan.

"Keep the same distance from the U-boat as we are now since they've obviously not spotted us," the Captain said. He turned toward the communications officer, "see if we also get a copy of the response."

The officer saluted and left.

"My priority is the safety of this ship and everyone aboard," said Captain Joyce. "Your uncle has been reassured by the German

Naval Command that the *Baltic Queen* would not be attacked on its way to the designated Polish port in Danzig, but we can't be sure that this information has trickled down to all the right people. There was no such guarantee given for our escorts. I guess they thought we should come alone and their word should be good enough."

"I've heard it said that there's always a lone gunslinger out to add a notch to his six-shooter," Stefan said.

"Right you are, but disobeying German Naval Command is another way of committing suicide," said the Captain. "I must get to the bridge. We don't want our co-ordinates to change in any way. So far, there is no indication that the U-boat is aware of us."

"Will you let me know the German Naval Command's response if we're lucky enough to pick it up?" asked Stefan.

"Of course." Captain Joyce knew that he was commander of the *Baltic Queen*, but Stefan Zurowski had the authority to make suggestions or even decisions. Jósef Zurowski had directed it to be so. The old man couldn't make this trip, but it wouldn't have been possible without him.

Stefan Zurowski, Jósef's nephew, had Captain Joyce's respect. He had fled Poland to America to carry out a mission, and Captain Joyce had been proud to be a part of it. Stefan Zurowski wasn't the same man now. His resolve had been hardened, but his love for his new family had tempered him from becoming bitter. Now, he was a force to be reckoned with as he fought his own personal battle with the Nazis.

The *Baltic Queen* again received a bounced communique from the German Naval Command to their U-boat: *Permission granted for the U-boat to destroy the merchant ship. Communications cut off. No help will be forthcoming.*

"So, what shall we do, Captain?" Stefan questioned after he had read the communique.

"Hold steady and keep our positions," answered Captain Joyce. "When the attack is over, the U-boat may be called away to join a 'wolf pack' going after a convoy, but it sounds as if it will be left alone to any fate it encounters. This is a renegade boat and crew separated either by chance or by choice."

"Is there any way to warn the merchant ship?" asked Stefan.

"Not without making our presence known, but we might be able to send a request to the Registrar General of Shipping and Seamen. For security reasons they no longer require crew lists or ship's logs, but it's still mandatory to record the movements of merchant vessels."

"I know you had to register our route and destination," said Stefan.

"Yes, crew members and passengers for the *Baltic Queen* had to be recorded along with our destination. The non-listing guidelines cover only the merchant ships," explained the Captain.

"Can we radio back and ask if any Allied merchant ship planned to use the shipping lane that we're using?"

"A message sent back to our home port might not be monitored; but our escort ships and plane can't be contacted because it would signal their existence which, so far, doesn't seem to be known," said the Captain. "We were given a few code words and a special frequency to use. If we only use it once, it might not be picked up, and it should seem innocent enough."

"Let's do it," said Stefan. "Inquire if an Allied merchant ship was expected to be in our shipping lane heading to our destination. I am going to tell my family about this situation. I don't want to keep any secrets from them. They all came willingly, and I have to respect that."

Stefan left the Captain and went to join his family for lunch. Quickly, he told them what he and Captain Joyce had learned from the intercepted messages, and he told them they were waiting for a response for the origin of the merchant ship.

"Can't we have our escort plane bomb the U-boat when it surfaces?" asked Ish.

"No, we can't message them for fear of our signal being picked up," answered Stefan. "And so far, our escorts' presence has been cloaked. They'll only respond in a defensive mode."

"So, let's do it ourselves!" Monica's eyes flashed. "Don't we have torpedoes onboard?"

"We do have. And they are equipped with the latest guidance system available, but this would require that we get close enough and we might be spotted," explained Stefan.

"Isn't there the chance that the U-boat might find us after they take out the merchant ship?" asked Sophia, fearfully. "The boys…."

"Yes, my dear, we're all at risk," Stefan said. He would pull no punches. They had a right to fear.

"The *Baltic Queen* was assured safe passage, but this seems to be a renegade ship reluctant to follow the rigid protocol of the German navy. I don't think its Captain will be getting a promotion for this," Stefan's voice was heavy with sarcasm.

"Can we vote?" Monica wouldn't give up.

"Vote?" asked Stefan.

"Yes," she retorted. "Since we're all in jeopardy, maybe we should all have a say in whether or not to risk an attack?"

"I don't think any of us want to see the merchant ship destroyed," agreed Ish.

Manka and Stanislas were sitting quietly, not joining in the conversation. But the expressions on their faces showed they did have opinions.

"Ok. Manka. Stanislas. What are you thinking? asked Stefan.

"I'll vote with Ish. Whatever he says," Manka looked at her new husband with trust.

"Ok. Stanislas?"

"I'm not a family member, but I am on this ship," he chuckled. "I attended the briefing explaining all the advanced technology installed on this ship. If the Captain agrees that we can destroy the U-boat as it surfaces and before it knows we're behind it, then this might be our best choice. The communique did say 'no help will be forthcoming', so it sounds as though the commander sending the message was leaving this lone wolf to suffer any problem that would arise."

"It's a risk," Sophia was still reluctant. "But we can't chance the U-boat finding us."

"True, my dear," said Stefan.

"It's a gamble either way. It might be better to be on the offensive," added Ish.

"We'll put it to a vote. I'll tell the captain our decision and see if he has any reservations," said Stefan.

The vote was unanimous. Even Sophia agreed with the others as to the wisdom of their choice. Their destiny lay in Poland and any obstacle must be removed.

The sun slipped below a cloud and was swallowed quickly by a hungry sea. Twilight would soon turn to dusk when there would no longer be any sunlight, reaching the time for the U-boat to surface and send the helpless merchant ship into the depths of the Atlantic.

The torpedoes had been positioned. The guidance system had searched and locked on to the U-boat's position. Calculations were run to pinpoint the exact spot where the U-boat would need to surface in order to take out the merchant ship.

Captain Joyce admired the courage of those on board and had agreed that this was the best plan. Anxiety was a tangible thing as they stood together awaiting the Captain's order to fire. The captain saw that Stefan Zurowski's face was devoid of the concern he must be feeling, and the disquiet of those around him would do nothing to ease his fears.

"Steady as she goes," the captain spoke to the crew, "but be alert."

All eyes strained to see through the gathering darkness. The clouds were darkening and the waves tried to mount to meet them.

"There it is," the captain whispered, as a dark form rose from the waves.

It was narrow and at least 200 feet long. An ocean-depth predator stalking its prey. A stray shaft of light escaped through the clouds and bounced silver off its side.

"Fire!"

Gasps could be heard at the suddenness of the command.

As the red flames lit the sky from the explosion destroying the U-boat, the merchant ship could be seen sailing safely away. She would reach her destination without ever knowing to whom she owed her escape.

"Well, done, Captain Joyce," Stefan breathed a sigh. "Shout out our thanks to your crew!"

"Yes, indeed," said the Captain, "and give an 'all's well' to our escorts. They'll definitely deserve an explanation later."

Tension floated away on the sounds of their laughter.

"Maybe we'd better wait to tell Jósef about this when we get home," Stefan said.

"Good idea," Ish agreed. "I'm not sure his heart could stand it. I think mine may have skipped a beat or two."

Their adrenalin ebbed as they watched the last pieces of the U-boat sink out of sight. Shudders came with thoughts of what might have been. Shoulders sagged as they made their way to their quarters, hoping that sleep would come to wipe out the destruction they'd witnessed.

Stefan's last thought was a prayer. *Thank you, Lord, for your protection and the new equipment we have onboard.*

Chapter 7

Stefan took in the devastation around him. The damage in Danzig that had started as he fled Poland had been completed. Hardly a building could boast of having more than two walls. Burned-out vehicles were abandoned but looked like they had been providing shelter for some.

He watched culture shock take hold of those he'd brought with him from the safety of America. The look on Ish's face registered as a blow to his gut, and Manka, wide-eyed, held on to his arm. Stefan knew Ish had seen Danzig many times, but these new memories would overshadow those of his youth and would be with him until the end of his days.

Sophia and Monica huddled together protecting Konrad between them, Sophia clutching tightly to Jan. They'd dressed as refugees before leaving the ship, and the shock on their faces would be assumed to have been put there by earlier scenes. No one would be suspicious.

Frederic was the first person Stefan saw when they disembarked from the *Baltic Queen*. The years fell away as he embraced his friend.

"Stefan, you're looking well. And, if I may say so, you look much like your father," Frederic said.

"You may say so, Frederic, but I hope that is where the similarity ends," said Stefan. Their laughter blended. "Let me introduce you to my wife, Sophia, the love of my life, and our two sons, Konrad and Jan." He tried to keep his tone light in the face of the surrounding devastation. He had done his mourning. Now was his time to act.

The family hurried after Stefan. Konrad held tightly to his father's hand, but he didn't seem fearful of the ruin around him. His eyes wandered to a group of small boys who stood staring at the newcomers.

Sophia slipped her hand into Frederic's outstretched one. She saw tears on his face as he looked at her and the child she held.

"What a privilege to see you," said Frederic.

Stefan finished the introductions of his fellow travelers to Frederic and turned to the business at hand.

"We need a place to steady our legs," he said, "and to clear up some seasickness. To his own chagrin our doctor suffered most of the trip."

"I've been able to secure a house for us, and it will be a suitable place to unwind and rest for all of you while *The Baltic Queen* is being unloaded. I've marked a map for our caravan's route, and I've hired men to accompany us as guards," said Frederic. "Many things here are in short supply, and some people are desperate. I've stationed men in strategic places along our route to secure the area. They're being paid well enough to be trusted. They got half their money when I hired them, and we'll pay them the rest as we pass their designated areas."

"Ever thoughtful. Ever efficient. Frederic, I can't thank you enough," said Stefan, clapping the man on his shoulder.

"Kasia insisted upon coming with me to meet you all. She has a meal waiting for us. She's also been preparing food for our journey."

They walked with Frederic the short distance from the waterfront to a house. It looked to be the only house to survive the devastation, but it was plain to see that things were coming alive once more.

Manka and Kasia immediately bonded through their love of feeding people. Manka helped Kasia put steaming bowls of food on the table. The fare was plain but plentiful.

Konrad's head drooped to the table, and his eyes closed. Sophia followed Kasia through the kitchen and up the stairs to a second floor where the boys would sleep. They were tucked into their beds, and the women joined the group that had moved into the parlor.

"Stefan, I didn't tell you before, but immediately after you left, I went back to the estate. When it was dark, a few workers and I slipped in and buried your family. The soldiers had no interest in the happenings at the family cemetery," Frederic's voice cracked. "They were just glad the bodies were out of their way."

"Frederic, you don't know how much that means to me," said Stefan.

"When we moved to the estate, we planted flowers on the graves," Kasia added. "They'll be in bloom soon."

"Thank you, Kasia," said Sophia.

It was late and everyone was ready for a bed that wasn't rocking by waves. Kasia directed each to where they would rest for the night. Stefan and Sophia were to share a bed in the room where Jan now slept. The house wasn't large and rooms had to be shared. Cots lined the walls in the parlor where the remaining could rest for the night. Shared accommodations were a luxury; people outside still had to find places to sleep on the streets.

Monica would sleep in the bed with Konrad. She tiptoed into the room trying not to awaken him. He might want his 'Aunt Monkey' to tell him a story, and she was just too tired. Reaching the bedside she raised the cover to slip under. His cover was bunched up in the bed, but the boy wasn't there.

"Sophia," Monica said as she tapped lightly on the door to Sophia and Stefan's bedroom. "Did Konrad come in there with you?"

"No," Sophia answered, "we put him in your bed."

"He isn't in the room with me now," Monica said, her voice urgent.

Stefan opened the door quickly. He was still dressed. "What do you mean he isn't there?"

"Not in the room anywhere, and there's a blanket missing from the bed," Monica's hand clutched at her chest. "Stefan, find him."

"Calm down, Monica, I'm sure he woke up and wanted to look around. You know how curious he is," Stefan's words didn't mask his unease. Sophia now stood behind him, clasping his arm.

"Where's Konrad, Monica?" shouted Sophia. "We put him in your room."

"I don't know, Sophia," Monica defended. "He wasn't in my room when I came up to bed." A sob escaped her as she leaned against the door.

"Stefan, what is it?" Frederic stood at the foot of the stairs with a lighted candle.

"Konrad doesn't seem to be in his room or anywhere upstairs," said Stefan.

"I'll look down here," Frederic said. He turned and hurried through the house.

Frederic checked with the man guarding the front of the house, and there had been no disturbance. He went back through the kitchen to the porch. There, it was obvious that the door had been forced open.

The guard at the back of the house was lying on the porch floor, he had been stabbed.

"Stefan, come quickly," Frederic said. He knelt beside the man, holding his light above the lifeless figure.

"Let the doctor look," Stefan said, nodding to Stanislas.

Stanislas knelt beside the man, checked for a pulse in his neck, then looked at Stefan and shook his head. "The body isn't cool to the touch yet; rigor mortis has begun its onset, so I'd say the man has been dead a little over three hours. The knife had been plunged directly into the heart, and he would have bled out immediately."

"None of us heard anything, but it must have happened while we were gathered in the parlor farthest from the back door," said Frederic.

"We need to call the police?" asked Monica.

"There are no police here, Monica," answered Frederic. "This is just another war victim. This one will be luckier than most, as he died quickly. The other guards will remove him and notify his relatives," said Frederic, "if he has any still left alive."

Frederic knelt beside the doctor and took the folded paper that was tucked into the front of the dead man's coat. He quickly scanned its contents and turned a stricken face to the group behind him. With blurred vision, he stretched a pleading hand to Stefan. "I've failed you. We won't find your son in the house."

Sophia moaned softly, and Stefan caught her before she could slump to the floor.

Chapter 8

From the circle of light around the lantern now sitting on the table, Stefan could read the contents of the note to those gathered around him.

Count Zurowski, you have done well so far. We took your son to assure us of your continued cooperation. Whether you have the item for exchange with you or secreted at your estate, your son will remain with us until the trade. His well-being depends on you. Our troops will be joining your guards on the journey as far as Danzig. A special ambassador from our Fuhrer will meet you there at Domani z Camin.

It was signed *NAC, bearing the swastika.*

"What's NAC?" asked Stanislas.

"NAC stands for the Nazi Art Committee," answered Frederic, "and the swastika is an ancient religious icon. The icon is said to bring prosperity and peace. Such symbols are often found in archeological excavations. Hitler particularly covets artifacts that are said to have occult properties. Later a right-facing swastika was adopted by the Germans, symbolizing a superior Aryan race."

"Well, isn't that just Hitler's hang-up? What does this have to do with us?" asked Monica.

"We have such an artifact, but we've tried to keep it secret," answered Stefan.

"Why kidnap Konrad? Can't they just steal it from us?" wailed Monica.

"They can't take it by force. They tried that while we were in America, and they failed. The NAC is now convinced it must be handed over willingly, otherwise a curse will fall on the new owners," explained Stefan.

"Hey, am I the only one who doesn't know about this?' she asked.

"I didn't know," said Stanislas, looking at Monica.

"But you aren't family," she retorted, turning her back on him.

"It isn't talked about, so only a few of us know," Stefan said, ignoring Monica's outburst. "It's going to be a long time before dawn, and perhaps the story will be best coming from Frederic. He was the first one to tell me. It won't take our minds off of Konrad, but it's an important part of the Zurowski legacy." Stefan turned to Frederic, "do you mind?"

Frederic nodded in agreement and settled back into his chair.

He began softly, "The early enemies of the Polish were the Prussians. The German Knights of the Teutonic Order had been invited by Konrad, Piast Duke of Mazowsze, to help the Knights of the Teutonic Order undertake missionary work among the Prussians on the northeastern borders of Poland. How was Poland to know she invited in a group that was to become a far greater threat than the Prussians? The Knights of the Teutonic Order lived and headquartered in Malbork Castle."

"We'll pass Malbork Castle on the way to Domani z Camin," interrupted Stefan.

"Yes, I believe that many have taken refuge there away from their bombed-out villages," Frederic added, then continued. "The Teutonic knights settled and extended their authority along the Baltic Coast. Later, the Teutonic knights merged with an aggressive missionary order called the Knights of the Sword. The ascendancy of the Zurowski family began with their part in the Polish-Lithuanian victory over the combined forces of the German knights at Grunwald. The grandmaster of the Teutonic Order himself surrendered and paid homage to the king of Poland, and the king honored a few of the valiant warriors; Konrad Zurowski was one of the most zealous patriots. The king of Poland bestowed upon him a captured estate, and Konrad Zurowski took the name of the king to add to his own: the first Count Konrad Piast Zurowski came into being. Generation after generation of descendants gave the revered name Piast to the firstborn son. After the Battle of Grunwald, the Teutonic Order survived only as a weak religious organization."

"You're right. It doesn't take my mind off of Konrad," said Monica, sighing deeply.

"No, but maybe it will help you understand why the NAC has been told of its mysterious value," said Stefan, "so let Frederic go on with the story."

Frederic paused as he attended to the simple chore of polishing the lenses in his round steel-rimmed glasses with his soft white handkerchief, methodically cleaning each lens in a careful circular motion until the glass sparkled in the dim light. When he put his spectacles back on, his high, scholarly forehead creased as though he were reaching back into his thoughts for the age-old remembrance.

He continued, "Ansback, the last grandmaster disbanded the German Knights of the Teutonic Order and made their possessions and lands into a hereditary fief for his own family. But an old priest within the order had a little band of followers who bravely opposed the grand master. The priest's handful of friends were killed, and he was forced to flee for his life. He found refuge at Domani z Camin, Count Zurowski's castle. The count was a very brave and devout Catholic. For months, the grandmaster searched the forests and watched the castle, but he was finally forced to admit defeat and abandon the hunt. On his deathbed, the priest said that he wished to atone for the wrong the knights had done to Poland. He wanted the count, as a descendant of the patriot Zurowski at Grunwald, to have the crucifix for the wrongs perpetrated against the Polish people. The priest's anger was hot against the grandmaster for abandoning religious endeavors. His final reason for giving the count the priceless crucifix was that the Polish gentry was strongly against the Protestant influence making itself felt at the time, threatening a schism. At his death, he was buried in the Zurowski family plot.

"So, what does this crucifix look like and where is it?" asked Monica.

Stefan's face glowed in the light as he answered the question, "the crucifix is eight inches tall. The golden cross is outlined in intricate gold filigree. The figure of the crucified Christ is skillfully carved from warm, glowing ivory and mounted on the face of the cross. Each thorn amid the emerald leaves that encircle the crown on his head is a black pearl, and the wounds on his body are rubies. The blood drops from the wounds are tiny rubies. The back of the crucifix is encrusted with jewels and the edges of the cross are set with rubies, matching the blood drops on the Christ figure on the cross."

"So, this is the ransom demanded for Konrad's freedom?" asked Stanislas, raising his brows at Stefan.

"Yes, they want the crucifix," he admitted.

"Well, where is it?" asked Monica.

"It's safer for you not to know. But I can get hold of it, and we *will* get my son back," Stefan's words were forced through tight lips. "In America, the NAC sent someone to get it, but they failed. So, this is a desperate tactic. Hitler feels his power slipping, and he is looking for spiritual backing. Three years ago, in 1941, the Battle of Moscow showed him that he wasn't invincible. Actually, that was the first defeat suffered by Nazi Germany."

Stefan stood, signaling a change of subject. "Not a soothing bedtime story, but let's try to get a little sleep. The trip to Domani z Camin will be grueling." He climbed the steps to the bedroom where Sophia slept with Jan. He needed to touch them.

Chapter 9

Dawn was only a subtle hint in the early morning sky. Stefan and Sofia were seated at the table waiting for Frederic and the others to join them. They sipped from the steaming mugs of coffee for comfort as well as warmth. Sweetened pastries completed their breakfast.

"Sophia, are you alright now?" asked Stephan. Their eyes met and held. "I wish I could take your pain."

"Oh, Stefan, please don't worry about me," she said. "I was exhausted but now I'm not so fragile. I won't disappoint you again."

"Sophia, you could never disappoint me."

"We'll do what they say, and they'll bring Konrad back," she said. Her hand trembled as she placed her cup down, spilling coffee over the edge.

"He won't be brought back, Sophia, we'll get him back when we deliver the crucifix to them at Domani z Camin. Someone will be waiting for us there," Stefan explained.

"Can we trust them?"

"We have no choice. But I've warned them of the curse that will fall upon them if they fail to return Konrad or harm him in any way," said Stefan.

"Can you do that?" Her expression was suspicious, "is that true?"

"There is a rite for that. It's explained in the writings that the old priest left when he presented the crucifix to old Count Zurowski," said Stefan. "It's never been used, but it sends out a powerful threat to those who are already superstitious."

The back stairs creaked as Frederic made his way into the kitchen, pouring himself a mug of coffee and sitting opposite Stefan.

"As soon as it's light enough to see, we can make our way to the *Baltic Queen* and see to the offloading of our cargo," said Frederic. "It wouldn't be safe to try to find our way in the dark."

"I imagine that we'll have an escort even if we can't see them. I doubt if the NAC will let us out of their sight until we reach Domani z Camin," said Stefan.

"Our trip will be as safe as we can make it with double guards," said Frederic. "The resistance fighters know of our presence here and will pretend to ignore us." He refilled his coffee mug and took a sip before continuing, "a member of the underground slipped in here about three hours ago and took Ish with him. He and his escort left disguised as Catholic priests. Once in Warsaw, they'll be met by resistance fighters in the surrounding forest. The Jewish Fighting Organization is unified there and have underground tunnels and bunkers. Some had escaped deportation to the Treblinka extermination camp through the sewers. If at all possible, they'll get Ish safely to the other side of Warsaw; as they are aware of the supplies the Zurowskis sent that were smuggled into the ghetto, and they know that Ish was involved, too. From there, he and the priest will be on their own as they travel north."

"With the SS still on the lookout for Jews that escaped the Warsaw Ghetto, Ish thought he might be a danger to us all," said Stefan. "I wanted to talk him out of leaving us, but I knew he was right. He said he was leaving Manka in our care."

"He will be safer once they reach the other side of Warsaw. The areas between there and Domani z Camin aren't well-populated but they still won't travel in broad daylight. We've been granted passage; except we'll have to wear these armbands for identification at least until we get through Warsaw. We can take the back roads with our trucks and our dozer; the well-traveled roads are too rough from the bomb damage," said Frederic.

"At least they're not black like the SS wear," said Stefan as he slipped the red band over his sleeve. "These bands actually bear Hitler's signature, and if we want to keep control of our caravan, we'd better not be caught without them."

"We won't be able to keep from drawing attention," said Frederic.

"We may have to let the bulldozer clear our path some of the time," said Stefan.

"Yes, it will be rough on the trucks and the tractor," agreed Frederic, "and we certainly don't want to have to stop and fix a tire."

Sophia listened to the talk, taking strength from the conversation. "What can we do to help? All I can think of is Konrad. I need something to do!"

"Kasia plans to prepare all the food that we were able to bring. We'll need to take some of it, and we'll leave the rest of it in this house. She can keep you busy. She'll need help. And we must leave the house with no evidence of who we are or where we're headed," said Frederic.

Stefan interrupted, "you must do everything as quietly as possible. Draw no attention to yourselves. I know we talked about this last night but please remind Monica it's for our safety."

"What about Jan? How can I keep him quiet?' Sophia squeezed her hands tightly in front of her.

"Stanislas will stay here, and if necessary, he can give him a sedative," explained Stefan. "He came prepared for this."

"Oh, Stefan," cried Sophia. She took comfort in the arms he wrapped around her.

"You'll manage, my love," said Stefan.

"I know you left most of your belongings on the boat. That's good. But we'll leave the food stuff here when we leave. We can't see them, but I know there are those waiting to descend upon this house when we leave. Food and clothing are in short supply," said Frederic.

"The last week of sailing, Ish and Manka prepared food while we were on the boat. It's stored in one of the trucks and should see us through until we get to Domani z Camin," said Sophia. "Nothing perishable, of course; but there's powdered milk to be made for Jan."

"Follow Kasia's plan so we can be ready to leave as soon as we arrive with our caravan," said Frederic. "Hopefully, no later than noon."

As the others joined them in the kitchen, there was a light tap on the back door. "Ok, Stefan, they're here. Ready? It shouldn't take long for the crew to offload the *Baltic Queen*."

Stefan kissed Sophia, held her for a moment, and then followed Frederic out into the morning twilight.

Chapter 10

It was full light as they made their way through the rubble that disguised the streets of Danzig. The sun allowed its brightness to expose the devastation at every turn, but it offered no warmth on this early spring day. Frost sparkled from a tall metal steeple standing in defiance.

The Nazi's first blitz had caused major devastation in Danzig the day before Stefan left for America. Now he saw total destruction: wooden structures splintered and charcoaled, metal twisted in macabre shapes throwing long, threatening shadows. Down the alleyways, he could see people huddled by small campfires. It was May, and the mornings were still cool. They had boarded the *Baltic Queen* in mid-April, and the ocean voyage had taken twenty days.

Captain Joyce met them and ordered the gangplank lowered. "Mornin' guys," he greeted, stretching out his hand to first Stefan and then Frederic. "It's been unusually quiet during the night, so I think that's a good sign. The crew is ready to do whatever you need."

"Thanks, Captain. We'll be quick because I know that you need to start back as soon as possible. Our cargo has been secured in the trucks, and they just need to be driven off," said Stefan.

They greeted the crew, then watched as the three canvas-covered trucks lumbered down the gangplank followed by the tractor and the bulldozer. Stefan knew that as they journeyed toward Warsaw, the bulldozer might be needed to make a path for the other vehicles. Their trek would be slow. He was also glad that the Nazis in Danzig and Warsaw knew of their importance to Hitler's plan. Their caravan would be as safe as it could be in this world of unrest.

Stefan thanked Captain Joyce, handing him a packet of letters to be given to Vincent Ludlow, their attorney in New York. Ludlow would see that it got to Uncle Jósef at Forest House. It would bring him up to date on their journey and arrival.

Stefan felt a sinking feeling of being cut loose on dangerous soil as the gangplank was pulled up and the boat immediately edged toward the open sea, back to the precarious situation on the waters.

What had he done? He'd brought his family here. No matter that Sophia had insisted they stay together. It didn't matter that they all came willingly. They had necessities in their possession that people would kill for. He felt the load for their safety.

"What have we done, Frederic?" Stefan asked Frederic as they sat together with the driver in the truck that would lead the way back to their borrowed house.

"I know, Stefan, I know," his sigh was deep. "You're doing what has to be done. Now, more than ever. We must get Konrad back. Sophia is holding up well for the present, but it's wearing on her."

Quietness descended in the cab, each lost in their own thoughts.

Stefan was aware that the Nazis began a pogrom against the Jews before he left Poland. He knew that the first concentration camp was established thirty miles from Danzig at Stutthof. It had been immediately built after he escaped in 1939. When he left, the Danzig Synagogue had already been burned out by the Nazis in November the year before. In 1939 when he'd come through Danzig, he'd seen a tattered banner flapping in the wind announcing, 'The Synagogue Is To Be Destroyed'. It had been gutted by fire, five years ago now. He and Uncle Jósef had fought the battle for their homeland from the shores of America, but now he'd come back to restore Domani z Camin.

He remembered seeing the *Schleswig-Holstein* in Danzig's harbor the night before he was smuggled aboard the *Baltic* Queen. It had fired on a Polish munitions' depot. Germany's first blitz was experienced in Danzig. This intense military campaign was so successful that it was used against the United Kingdom where the term blitzkrieg was first used by the British press to define the intense bombing campaign. Danzig was still under the control of the Nazis, and he and his party were safe only because they had a powerful bargaining chip--the crucifix: something the German Fuhrer wanted. Now that the Nazis held Konrad hostage, he would wade through perdition to get it to them and redeem his son.

As the caravan started away from the harbor, the trucks traveled slowly, bouncing over debris, and bombed-out ruts. Stefan didn't see the guards that Frederic had hired to travel with them, but he knew they were well-skilled in the art of camouflage. These men had lost everything with the bombing in Danzig and would remain at Domani z Camin to start rebuilding their lives. Stefan hoped the estate would provide sanctuary for many. Although the Polish guards were out of sight, the SS who were mounted on motorcycles didn't try to hide their presence.

The trucks rumbled to a stop in front of the house that Frederic had procured for them. The travelers were ready and waiting. To any onlookers, those leaving the house and entering the trucks could be any small group that was being transported to who-knew-where. Clothed as refugees, their few belongings carried in cloth bags over their shoulders, they pulled themselves up into the back of the canvas-covered vehicle. Stefan knew that Kasia had provided the proper clothing for each of them, and the women had dark scarves on their heads tied securely under their chins. Their party blended in with those wandering the streets. The travelers had become somber, heads down, and no one was talking. Mostly, he knew their thoughts were of Konrad. Was he cold? Was he hungry?

"Frederic, how long will it take us to get to Warsaw?" Stefan broke the silence. He was driving one of the trucks, and it took most of his concentration to keep it in the road.

"It's 425 km," Frederic said.

"Ok, roughly 265 miles, so hopefully we can get there before dark even on these roads," Stefan said. "I hate the Nazi motorcycle escort surrounding us."

"They'll be with us until Warsaw. From there, we may be on our own. I'm not sure even these Nazi guards want to expose themselves to the freedom fighters hiding in the forests surrounding Warsaw. Many of them are Jews that escaped being taken to camps and have joined with the Poles. They have nothing more to lose and will fight to the death."

"Well, we did leave early enough to make it by dark if just barely," said Stefan.

"The accommodations will be rough for the women," said Frederic. "We'll have to make a campfire and spend the night in the trucks. It will be safer for us and all of our goods. I couldn't get any place for us to stay."

"Don't apologize, my friend. Manka and Sophia won't complain. And Monica wouldn't dare. I threatened not to bring her with us, but she said she wanted to help Sophia with the boys," said Stefan. "Frederic, will we need to take turns guarding our camp?"

"No. The men I hired will, but they'll form a hidden periphery around our camp. We'll not see them, but they'll see us. And we've other men with us. The other truck drivers and the one operating the bulldozer. All armed I suppose?"

"Yes," said Stefan. "All armed. Even Stanislas and our women are armed. Uncle Jósef made sure of that."

They traveled in silence for the next few hours until Warsaw came into sight.

"Count Zurowski." It was one of the motorcycle riders, riding up to the window on the driver's side.

"Yes, what is it?" asked Stefan.

"Here is where we leave you. Someone will be at Domani z Camin to make our trade. Make no mistake. We have the boy, and his life means nothing to us," he laughed. "Actually, less than nothing."

The man was still laughing as he turned his motorcycle back toward Danzig followed by the other three who had ridden with him. The debris from the wheels as the motorcycle spun out struck the metal of the truck, sounding like gunfire.

Stefan hoped Sophia hadn't heard the threat. The tightness in his chest threatened to cut off his breathing.

Chapter 11

His rabbi would chuckle if he could see him now. It had been a long time since he'd been to temple, so his rabbi might be glad to see him in any costume. Ish pulled up the hood on the monk's robe he wore as he settled down for the night. His traveling companion was a genuine Catholic priest, and Ish could hear the man whispering his prayers to the rattle of the rosary. They'd eaten bread and cheese again, washing it down with water from a nearby spring. Now they hunkered down in a small, dry cave they'd found and felt safe for the night.

"It's time to go," it was a whisper that echoed in the small cave where Ish and the priest had slept. Dawn had yet to break. The hooded figure had a small penlight that beckoned to them.

"Ready," Ish answered for both of them.

"I have a rope. Both of you hold to it as I lead. We'll move slowly and as quietly as we can," the man continued to speak in whispers. "I'm leading you to a tunnel that comes out in the forest. There are no guards there."

"We'll be going north," said Ish. "Can you tell us anything about guards there?"

"Even guards don't want to go there. You'll have to watch out for swampy bogs and snakes. It does get better further north. Don't tell me where you're going, though. What I don't know I can't be forced to tell."

Ish's boots came to his knees, so he felt protected from snakes. He didn't know if the priest had suitable footwear or not. He hoped he never had to find out.

Nothing more was said until they got to the mouth of the tunnel, covered by a tangle of brush. After Ish and the priest entered, their escort re-covered the tunnel's entrance, leaving them alone. After going a few feet into the tunnel, Ish pulled his flashlight from his pack to see their surroundings. The floor was packed dirt, and the walls and ceilings were slick with oozing water. To save his batteries, Ish turned off his light and they slowly moved forward.

"We will go on by faith in God," the priest murmured.

"Ah, yes, God," said Ish. *But where is the God of Abraham, Isaac, and Jacob in all of this? I don't like being alone with my thoughts, but I'm sure my thoughts aren't like the priest's thoughts. He must be thinking quite a lot because he isn't much of a talker.*

Their guide had said that the tunnel went about a mile outside of Danzig, and Ish guessed that they'd been walking about twenty minutes. There were times that he had to shine his light on the path as they were forced to stumble over rocks.

He saw a shaft of light reaching in from the end of the tunnel. Light. He had always hated darkness. He thought suddenly of Manka, the light of his life. He had always loved her brightness and her shining countenance. He hoped time spent here didn't darken her soul.

They walked more quickly to the light, but then stopped. Ish peered cautiously into the woods surrounding them. No one was in sight. He nodded to the priest, and they both stepped out of the tunnel.

They found a dry, grassy spot under a tree and sat down.

"Shall we have some refreshment?" asked the priest.

"Guess it's time for breakfast," agreed Ish. "I think it's bread and cheese again."

"Many times, I've had only a small piece of bread," said the priest. "Thank you for sharing your cheese." The hand he extended was thin and trembled slightly. The journey would be hard on this man. Ish knew he would be forced to travel more slowly than he'd intended. He took an apple from his knapsack and handed it to the priest.

"We'll share," the priest said. He broke the apple into two pieces and handed Ish the larger half. Ish could hardly swallow for the lump in his throat. It had been so long since he'd been in want of any kind.

Ish took his compass from his knapsack. "We'll be heading northeast toward Olsztyn. Domani z Camin is a little further on.

"Ah, yes, Olsztyn, the home of the Olsztyn Castle, also known as the Warmian Bishops' Castle because bishops lived and ruled from there in another century," said the priest. "I've never been to Domani z Camin. Isn't that where the Zurowski lands are?"

"Yes, the new Count is returning to restore his land and find his people," said Ish. He stood, signaling the end of the conversation.

These were the most words the priest had spoken since they'd set out together. His words came out in a wheeze, so Ish could tell that the older man would need to save his breath for walking. He needed to share more of his food with the priest. He would have enough until he met up again with Stefan's caravan, even though the last stretch of their journey was still many miles. It would mean at least one more night where they would need to find shelter. They could make better time since it seemed safe now to travel during the daylight hours. They hadn't seen one person since they left the tunnel and entered the protection of the forest. With his compass he could keep them going northeast.

The bombing had been directed at Warsaw, so the outlying areas saw less destruction.

The priest had found a stick the right size to be used as a cane, and he was able to keep up with Ish. He had paced their walking for endurance rather than speed; they'd get there when they got there. If they did encounter anyone, it would be better to look like slow-moving stragglers rather than men on a mission. The sharp thorns had pulled at their long robes, so they did have a well-worn appearance.

They were able to make steady progress the entire day, and they'd only encountered one man on their journey. Ragged and wild-eyed, the man ran when he saw them, raising his hands into the air and screaming loudly. He had disappeared into the forest in a direction away from them. The priest stared after the man, crossing himself and moving his lips in silent prayer. No doubt many had been driven mad with fear and loss.

Again, they found a cave for the night. This one was a little larger, and Ish felt safe enough to build a small campfire at the back of the enclosure. The smoke seemed to be drawn upward and out through a small crack that exposed the twilight sky. Ish collected water from the stream that they'd been following, made coffee, and boiled some dried beef and salt for a thin broth. They dipped the hard bread into the broth and savored the warmth.

After they'd eaten and warmed themselves, Ish put out the fire with water and scattered the ashes, any smoke that would continue drifting up through the cave ceiling might raise suspicion if anyone passed by. Weary from walking, and warmed by the food and the fire, sleep came quickly.

The sound came softly at first. The moan might have been a bird of some kind. Then it came again louder, causing both the priest and Ish to awaken. Again, the moan came.

"Sounds like someone in pain," the priest said.

"You think the sound is human?" Ish asked, hoping the priest was wrong.

"I've heard such moans before," the priest said. "I must help." He struggled to get up.

"No, I'll go." Ish knew he could move more quietly alone.

He went to the mouth of the cave. Keeping the beam from his flashlight close to the ground, he skimmed his surroundings. The moan came again, and it seemed to be coming from the edge of the nearby stream where he saw what looked like a person huddled under a dark blanket.

Cautiously, he approached. When he got close, he shined his light on one of the figures that was a woman with the face of an angel. The child that she held close to her under the blanket continued to moan softly, then began to thrash around weakly.

"Sir, can you help her?" the woman asked, taking the chance that he might not be an enemy.

"Follow me." Ish picked up the child and carried her to the cave. The woman followed them to the back of the cave. The young woman settled with her back against a wall and again held the child close. Ish took the blanket he'd been using and laid it over the two. Gradually the woman stopped trembling, but the child continued to shake.

Ignoring the danger, the priest had started another fire and warmed some of the beef broth. He handed the cup of broth to the woman who took a sip and then tried to get a little down the girl's throat. The child moaned and turned her head.

"Miss, do you know what's wrong with the girl?" asked the priest.

"She'd fallen down a rocky embankment, but she thought she was ok. The gash on her leg has become inflamed. I cleaned it as best I could and soaked a cloth in the stream and bathed her face, but she's become feverish and slips in and out of consciousness" the woman said.

"Let me look," said Ish.

The woman uncovered the girl's leg, revealing red, puffy flesh around a gash.

"I think we've caught it in time. There aren't signs of blood poisoning yet, no red streaks running from the wound. I do have a first aid pack," said Ish. Manka had insisted that he take along a few medical supplies, telling him it would make her feel better if he had them.

The priest had boiled water, and the young woman bathed the wound while Ish assembled the bandage. When the wound was dry, the young woman applied a salve and bandaged it securely. He dissolved aspirin in water and helped the woman get it into the girl's mouth and saw her swallow. If she woke in the night, they'd give her more.

"That's all we can do," said Ish as he stood up. "Hopefully, she'll sleep quietly and be improved by morning."

"You don't look alike," said the priest "but is she related to you?"

"No. I found her after her fall. She told me her name is Sarah," the woman said.

"And who are you, my child, and where are you going?" the priest asked.

"My name is Leah," she answered. "My hometown was Jedwabne, but it was destroyed two years ago. I heard that Domani z Camin was abandoned and I'm going there to hide." She hoped they wouldn't ask her how she'd survived the massacre or where she'd been since she was taken from Jedwabne. A lie would be better than the truth. And a lie is all they'd get from her.

Ish gasped. If he weren't mistaken, this young woman was his niece. The face he saw in the dim light of the fire looked like the last picture his brother David had sent to him of his daughter. He'd written the name and age of Leah on the back of the picture. He'd said she'd finished her nurse's training, and the picture was of a beautiful blonde in a nursing uniform, smiling at the camera. He'd met David's wife some twenty years ago at their wedding, but Ish knew that her family hadn't been thrilled over their daughter's choice of husband. His wife had been a blonde-haired, blue-eyed beauty of Nordic descent without a hint of her Jewish heritage. She'd died giving birth to their only child.

"Here, try to get some more broth down Sarah, and maybe she'll rest for the night. I think we're safe here," said Ish, his hand trembled as he gave the cup to Leah.

There was so much he wanted to ask her, but there would be time. The most important thing now would be to join Stefan's caravan. Stefan would be looking for him and the priest after they were safely through Warsaw.

As Ish drifted to the edge of sleep, he thought perhaps he had seen the hand of the God of Abraham, Isaac, and Jacob at work. Or was this the hand of the Messiah that Stefan told him about?

Chapter 12

As Hitler's forces and endless lines of vehicles had made their way through Warsaw, the countryside and villages had been reduced to shapeless heaps of rubble. The road Stefan's caravan now traveled was banked on one side by collapsed buildings and on the other huge piles of rocks that had been moved aside. The bulldozer had moved in front of the trucks for the worst part of the trek through Warsaw.

"Frederic, much of the ghetto still stands," said Stefan. "I know the Nazis began liquidating the Warsaw Ghetto last year, but I heard the freedom fighters held out three weeks. We read, also, that only a year ago The Great Synagogue in Warsaw was blown up by one individual. I think it was SS-Gruppen Fuhrer Jurgen Stroop."

"Yes, this was the last act of destruction by the Germans in Warsaw, but I've heard Hitler says there won't be a Jew left in Europe by 1945," said Frederic. "From last report, the Warsaw Ghetto still houses thousands of people that had been rounded up from every village and shipped to this central location. It's been said that 7,000 Jews were killed in the uprising. Most burned to death. The army went on to flatten the city."

"Conditions must be unbearable," said Stefan.

"The Nazis have restricted rations deliberately. Some only get a cup of coffee and a cup of soup per day, so death from starvation isn't uncommon," said Frederic. "Some have found ways to escape and smuggle food back in. I've heard that a few have crawled through sewers to escape."

"The thousands who thought the trains were taking them to a refugee camp and away from this hell in the ghetto actually went to death camps," said Stefan. "I was told that often a prisoner would tell the guards about a planned rebellion, thinking he would get better treatment. It didn't help, and the informant was often gunned down with those staging the uprising. Bodies are left where they fall. The threat of typhus is rampant throughout the ghetto."

"But the uprising of the ghetto at Warsaw has given hope to other groups," said Frederic. "Prisoners escaping out to smuggle back food also brought back weapons. Nothing, of course, to rival the Nazis, but they did take out some of the guards. Usually after being told of a planned rebellion, the Nazi tanks would roll through the streets, firing destruction on houses and other buildings still standing. Young men were fighting for justice, fighting for the right to live. If not live, then die in a more *decent* way. Die looking death in the eye with determination if not tranquility."

The caravan had left Warsaw and was making its way on a make-shift road through the outlying forest. After they'd gone several miles, they seemed to be alone. The caravan pulled to a stop beside a stream. Fortunately, this part of Poland was replete with fresh-water streams.

Stefan walked to the back of his truck where Sophia and the others were riding.

"I think it's safe to get out and stretch your legs for a few minutes," he said as he helped the women get down from the truck. "Don't be long."

The women went off to relieve themselves in the shelter of the trees.

"Well, this is just another new experience for me," joked Monica. "But I can handle this." She took Jan from Sophia, so Sophia could have her hands free. "Definitely a different kind of bonding," Monica added.

"Oh, Monica," said Manka, "you are good for our spirits."

"And Stefan said I could be of no use," they all joined Monica's laughter.

Tension lifted and the women returned to the truck, smiles lifting some of the worry off their faces.

The drivers of the other trucks refueled the tanks and scraped the thick layers of dust from the windshields. Frederic and Stanislas had seen to refilling the water containers. Manka and Kasia had distributed food to each person. The rest stop was short, and they needed to make as many miles as possible before nightfall made traveling impossible.

Stefan took a few moments to be with Sophia and Jan before starting out again. He needed the reassurance that touching his family brought him.

"Everyone aboard? Time to head out," said Stefan. "Tomorrow we should meet Ish," He winked at a blushing Manka.

They met no one on the road as they traveled north. The villages had all been plundered. Charcoaled beams lay where they'd collapsed, but the ashes were long cold. There was nothing left to sustain life. The inhabitants who'd lived here may have been taken to the multi-storied Warsaw Ghetto where they faced imprisonment, forced labor, starvation. Or extermination at Treblinka or another camp. A few had a prepared plan of escape.

Just before twilight's onset, they found a clearing large enough to provide space for the vehicles to form a semi-circle. The guards that Frederic had hired for the journey would now close in for another layer of protection behind the vehicles. These guards were well armed with the best that Uncle Jósef could furnish. In this land of upheaval, they were on as safe a ground as they could expect. They all still wore the red armbands bearing Hitler's signature, and they would keep them on until the trade was made for Konrad at Domani z Camin.

It was again a cold camp, but the food was plentiful and the water fresh. Jan's milk couldn't be warmed, but he seemed to be tolerating it. Even without the doctor's sedatives, the baby had been quiet during the journey. By tomorrow night, they might be far enough away from Warsaw to chance a fire if they still hadn't encountered any others on the road.

The women made pallets for sleeping on the floor of their truck. One of the other trucks had enough space on the floor for the men to stretch out for the night. Their muscles had taken a beating while fighting to keep the trucks on the road, and they faced another long drive tomorrow.

"I haven't been this crowded since sleeping in a tent at summer camp." Monica's voice and sounds of giggles could be heard from her truck.

Soon daylight ended, and the night sounds lulled the weary travelers to sleep. The guards would take shifts watching throughout the night.

Stefan bolted upright at the sound of knocking on his truck door. He grabbed his revolver and cautiously edged to the opening at the back of the truck. He could barely make out Ish in the pre-dawn light and lowered his gun.

"Ish!" Stefan exclaimed. He and the other men got out to meet him, "something wrong?"

"No, yeah, … maybe," Ish started.

"Well, what is it?"

"I found a child and a young woman. The child is hurt, and I think Stanislas should look at her," said Ish.

"You think it may be a trap?" asked Stefan.

Stanislas was already pulling his coat around him and grabbing his medical bag.

"No trap, Stefan. We saw no evidence of a trap, and the young woman was on her way to find a hiding place when she found the girl. I don't know what the young woman is hiding from, but she had heard that Domani z Camin was abandoned, and she was headed there. She told us her name is Leah and the child's name is Sarah."

Ish didn't know why he didn't tell Stefan he thought the young woman was his niece. Was it because he might be wrong? But the face of the young woman looked exactly like the last picture his brother had sent to him.

"Did she say where her parents are?" asked Stefan.

"She didn't say, and I didn't want to upset her."

"I'm ready," said Stanislas, peering again in his medical bag before snapping it closed.

"Ok. We'll stay here in camp until you return. Is it far?" asked Stefan.

"Not far. We'll try to be back in an hour. Leah can walk, but we will have to carry the girl," Ish said.

"How is the priest holding up?" asked Frederic. "He was injured when his church was destroyed."

"I'm sure he'll be glad to ride. He's getting weak," Ish said.

"Go. And get back as soon as you can," Stefan said. "I'm not sure we should stay in one camp too long."

Stefan watched until the two men were out of sight; then he walked back to the trucks.

"Everyone," he spoke softly, "silence may be our best defense.

Chapter 13

Early morning hadn't seen any improvement in Sarah. She no longer thrashed about, but her skin was hot and dry, and the wound looked angry.

"Father Nowak, I'll go find help and return as fast as possible."

"But who can help?"

"I have friends. Plans were made that we meet up with the caravan headed for Domani z Camin, and a doctor is traveling with them. The guards with them have been keeping their eyes out for signs of us. During the night, one of their guards slipped into our camp and said we'd meet up today. He told me how to get to their camp."

"Oh, I did not know," the priest sighed and settled back against the wall.

Ish knew that the priest had just about reached the end of his endurance, and the injured girl was in no condition to walk, so finding the trucks now so close was another God thing. He hurried out just as soon as it was light enough to see the path the guard had pointed out to him.

When he returned with Stanislas, Ish could see that the priest had tried to cover the mouth of the cave, but he had no trouble recognizing the entrance.

He pushed aside the brush and called in softly, "I'm back, and I've brought the doctor."

"Doctor, I've heated water," the priest said.

"Good, thank you."

"Stanislas, this is Sarah," Ish said as he knelt down beside her. "And this is Leah who found her."

When Ish leaned back, Stanislas saw Leah's face. An angelic face of beauty and purity, looking down on the young girl with compassion. He had to force his attention back to the injured child.

Sarah opened her eyes. "Are you going to help me?" she asked. "If it hurts, that's ok, I'm brave. I'm eight, you know."

"Sarah, I know you're brave. But I'm going to give you something that will keep me from hurting you. Will that be ok?" he asked.

"Sure, doctor," Sarah said.

He took a syringe from his bag and a vial of liquid. "This will stick just a bit, but soon you'll take a nap."

It was only a few minutes until her eyes closed.

Gently, Stanislas probed the wound. "I think there's something embedded that's got to come out," he said. "I can use some of that hot water."

From his medical bag, he selected antiseptic and sterilized a probe, a scalpel, and small forceps. With the sterilized scalpel, he made an incision on either side of the hard object that he could feel. Holding the lips of the wound open, he inserted the probe and moved into the incision. When he reached the object, he took the forceps and pulled it out.

"Gentlemen, this is a bullet. Looks like the child had more than an accident," Dr. Janda said.

"Leah, what can you tell us," Stanislas asked gently.

"Nazis were marching all the Jews from her village. When they neared a steep rocky embankment, Sarah said her mother pushed her down the hill and she hit her head on a rock," Leah answered.

"Obviously, the soldier shot her in case she was still alive," his lips tightened to a straight line. "But I think he intentionally shot her leg so she couldn't walk even if she regained consciousness and tried to climb up."

Stanislas finished cleansing the wound, closed it with a few stitches and put on a clean bandage. He washed and dried his hands and spoke harshly, "let's get out of here as soon as possible."

Father Nowak had doused the fire with water and scattered the ashes. The men's knapsacks were packed.

Stanislas could understand that Sarah wouldn't have anything, and Leah's small bag couldn't contain much. What was her story? He was glad that she was going to Domani z Camin with them, perhaps he could learn more. He wanted to know all about her.

The walk to where Stefan had stopped the caravan for the night was less than a half-mile. Sarah was a light burden, and Ish was able to carry her slight form without much effort. He handled her carefully, but the medicine that Stanislas had given her kept her asleep.

To make room for the new passengers in the back of the truck carrying the women, Manka moved to ride in the truck that Ish was now driving, leaving that driver to ride in the third vehicle. Kasia rode with her brother, Frederic, in the vehicle Stefan drove. No more overnight stops would be necessary; the overloaded conditions could be tolerated for a day. In a land with so much suffering, being crowded wasn't to be considered. Ransoming Konrad at the end of their destination was forefront in their minds. The thought of the three-year-old boy in the hands of the Nazis was never out of their minds.

Chapter 14

Ish and Manka rode in silence while he fought to control the vehicle, until they got to the place where the bulldozer had made the equivalent of a logging road. The potholes were filled and the road was now wide enough for the trucks to pass without scraping through the trees on both sides. This would make the last leg of their journey easier.

"Ish," Manka looked over at him.

"Yes?"

"I was worried for you. I don't want to lose you now," Manka blushed as she spoke unaccustomed words.

"No way. You made me wait long enough before you became my bride," he teased.

"Oh, be serious," she said.

"I am serious. It was a long wait." They laughed together.

"Ish, that young woman you brought back. Leah. I've seen her face somewhere, but I can't imagine where," Manka said. "Such a lovely girl."

"Do you think perhaps you've seen a picture of her?" he asked.

"That's it, a picture. Ish, she's your niece!" Manka said. "That's the girl in the picture you showed to me that your brother David sent just two years ago."

"My dear, do you see that, too?"

"Yes, but she's lovelier in person than in the picture. What a wonderful thing to find her now. Have you told her?" Manka asked.

"No. There's too much to say. Too much I want to learn from her. I think I'll have to go slowly. She seems vulnerable, and she hasn't volunteered anything about herself except that Jedwabne was her hometown. She didn't even offer her last name," Ish said. "I'm not sure she'd have told us her first name, except the priest asked her what her name was. I think it was a slip when she said she was looking for a place to hide."

"After Jedwabne, no wonder she would want to hide," sympathized Manka.

"But that's been almost two years ago. I think something has happened recently that has sent her into hiding," said Ish.

"We'll keep her safe. We'll protect her. She may be your only relative left."

"David's child. Oh, Manka, if it could only be true. But where is David? So very few people escaped the slaughter of Jedwabne."

"We won't give up hope until we know for sure," said Manka.

"You're what I need to keep my hopes up." He reached over and patted her leg.'

"Tell me about David. When was the last time you saw him?" Manka asked.

"I came back to Poland for David's wedding; he'd asked me to be his best man even after all those years apart. They were married in the Great Synagogue in Warsaw. Manka, I wish you could have seen that temple before it was destroyed. Four large round pillars in front with a menorah on each side on pedestals. The buildings stones were dressed, smooth and impressive. There was a cupola on top. I think it was bronze, but it may have been copper," Ish paused, then added. "Leonardo Marconi was the architect. He was quite well known."

"Oh, I wish I could've seen it," she said.

"Synagogues contain an ark, containing scrolls of the Law, and before the ark two candelabra, pews and a raised bimah. From this platform, scripture passages are read," he said.

"What a place for a wedding," she said, breathlessly.

"Her wealthy parents owned a bank and attended this synagogue. David was very good with figures and went to work in their bank. The worship, so I'm told, was in Polish rather than Yiddish. Quite modern for the time, I guess. For their wedding, the organ was played. It wasn't used for services but reserved for weddings. I was quite overcome. I didn't do anything to embarrass myself or David, but I sure felt out of place," he said. "When I did go to temple, it was a small one in a small village. I'm afraid you married a Polish peasant, my dear."

"Oh, Ish. You give yourself too little credit!" she said.

"Now on the whim of one man, it is gone. Destroyed completely." A flicker of hatred flashed across his face.

There was silence for only a few minutes, then Manka gently changed the subject.

"Tell me what David was like as a boy," Manka loved hearing Ish tell of his family. He was opening his heart to her.

"Handsome, smart, fearless and full of life. Growing up together was quite an adventure," said Ish, chuckling. "But we grew apart. David went off to university and I followed him two years later, but that wasn't for me. I liked working with my hands. Jósef Zurowski was graduated the year I arrived and I moved to Domani z Camin with him where we worked on the estate with his older brother, who was then Count Zurowski. Jósef was the second son with no real future on the estate. It seems like those sons born second are second-class citizens. Stefan met the same fate, except his father showed open disdain for him."

"But Stefan is such an exceptional young man," Manka protested.

"That he is, but his brother Konrad was born first. His mother had the misfortune to die giving birth to Stefan, and his father held him responsible."

"How hateful of him," Manka's face grew red.

"It's over, my dear," he chuckled at her protest. "Anyway, Jósef and I dreamed of moving to America. He wanted to be away from his brother. But it probably wouldn't ever have happened if it hadn't been for that jeweled crucifix."

"That crucifix seems to have a way of making things happen. I just hope it's enough to get Konrad back safely," she was angry.

"Don't worry, my dear, it will."

"Well, how did it force you and Jósef to leave?" she asked.

"Maybe force is too strong a word. Here's the story," he started.

"Oh, I've always wondered. Now we have time for you to tell me," she settled herself, trying to make the seat more comfortable.

"It was 1914, and I can remember exactly what happened and what was said," Ish began. "I, of course, wasn't invited to the dinner, but I was to be in the next room available if anything was needed. I stored it all in my memory."

"How awful," she protested. "Why weren't you invited?"

"It's not the way things were done," he said. "Hush, now, here's the story."

"Count Zurowski looked around at those at his table. He was a fortunate man. His countess had given him a son, his heir. Now they were expecting their second child, which would keep the title further away from his brother Jósef and the chance he would ever inherit. All was well. Plus, the count had a talisman to protect his future. He wasn't superstitious, but it had brought good fortune to the Zurowskis down through the years.

"The count sat at one end of the table with the countess at the other end. To his right sat his mother, the dowager countess, along with Jósef, his brother, and an unmarried older sister. To his left sat a widowed sister and the village priest and his nephew. The priest's nephew would never have been invited to such a dinner, but he was a visiting relative of the priest.

"'A toast to the countess on her birthday,' said the count. He lifted his glass, and they all turned to her. 'And in her honor, I will show the jeweled crucifix.'

"Reverently, he lifted an object from a velvet-lined box. The object seemed to catch fire and glisten, throwing splinters of color on the faces of those at the table. All eyes were on the golden crucifix embedded with jewels and a throbbing carving of the crucified Christ.

"Awe and reverence registered on seven of the faces. Greed gleamed in the eyes of the eighth."

"The dinner was over. 'Goodnights' were said, guests were not returning to their homes that night, so they were shown to their rooms, and the family retired for the evening.

"In the morning, the box that held the crucifix was empty. The talisman was gone," Ish finished.

"Who took it?" she asked, breathlessly.

"The priest's nephew had run away during the night, so it was always thought that he had stolen it. But it could never be proven, and the young man was never found."

"But he didn't take it?" she interrupted.

"Now, wait. You're getting ahead of my story," he laughed at her eagerness. "No, he didn't."

"Who did," she demanded.

"Jósef's grandmother, but her son never found out until Jósef wrote to him many years later. He had always been her favorite, so she was trying to even the score. She knew that Jósef and I were leaving for America the next morning. She helped Jósef finish packing and hid the crucifix among his things. He didn't discover it until we were in America," he said.

"Good for her," said Manka. "Did she get into trouble?"

"We never heard, but she was considered in her dotage and never given a thought. And upon her death, Jósef was given a large inheritance from the dowager. I don't suppose Jósef's brother had known about that or he would've tried to stop it."

"She was quite a woman!" Manka said. "And what a memory you have!"

"Well, it forever changed my life," he paused, then continued. "She loved Jósef and wanted him to have a chance. Jósef could borrow unlimited funds with the crucifix as collateral and build his own empire. I guess you could say he 'bought' Stefan to be his heir with the crucifix. The Count was more than happy to sell his second son to get the jeweled crucifix where he thought it belonged. Jósef loved his home at Domani z Camin, but there wasn't a place for him there. His move to America and proxy marriage to Sophia has turned out well, so you can say everything is good and was meant to be."

"And you helped him build this empire, step by step," she said.

"And you thought I was only good for growing flowers!" he teased.

"Oh, Ish, you're silly. I never thought that!" They laughed together.

"But now we're coming full circle," said Ish. "Once again the Zurowskis are depending on the crucifix. And we're back. Look, Manka, on ahead. There's the castle."

"Oh, Ish, did you come from a place such as this?" She was awe-struck.

"No, my dear, I only lived here for a few years with Jósef. I'm afraid my beginnings were much humbler," he answered.

"Oh, I'm so glad, or you wouldn't settle for a woman like me," she said.

"Well, fear not, my love. You are exactly right."

The Gothic structure stood in tribute to the old builders. In the Middle Ages, architects were simply called master builders and their names forgotten. The castle at Domani z Camin boasted grand arches, ornate windows, and flying buttresses holding up some of the loftier details.

But Ish remembered when he'd first seen the staggering sight of gothic detail in the interior of the edifice. The delicate vaulted ceilings seemed to reach up forever. The Knights Hall with a table large enough that there would always be room for one more. A suit of armor worn by the last Teutonic knight that died at the castle was displayed in an alcove. The late count, Stefan's father, had ruled his domain by an old rigid code, bending everyone's will to his.

The damage to the grounds did not diminish the grandeur of the red-orange brick fortress that cut against the blue sky, magnificent turrets, tile roofing, and the intimidating, impenetrable gate that had protected Zurowskis through generations.

When he and Jósef Zurowski had walked over the bridge of the moat years ago, the courtyard had been smooth and level, rolling gently to the entrance of the complex, back to the main gate of the castle, and then on back to the wide stairs at the entrance. They'd walked over the moat that surrounded the castle into their unknown future, and neither of them felt any regret.

The grass that had then been greening and well-tended was today rutted from the heavy military equipment that had raged through the area. It was dry here now, and the scene before them was one of ugly scars and disfigurement on the landscape. Not a welcome sight to come home to. He could only imagine the task of rebuilding that lay before Stefan.

Chapter 15

He'd been waiting for them to arrive. When the Nazi vehicle showed up, he saddled his horse and tied it nearby. He felt it might be necessary to give the expected arrivals a heads-up as to their new guest.

They must have seen him coming. The trucks stopped, ready and waiting for him to reach them.

"A touch of the old West," said Monica. "And what a hunk of a cowboy."

The rider was coming at a gallop to meet them, dust billowing as his horse's hoofs pounded the dry ground.

Not only had Monica weathered the rough trip and the horror they'd seen, but she had kept up her banter, lifting the spirits of those with her. She was struggling to keep her mind off of Konrad.

"Down, girl. You'll scare off the neighbor," said Stanislas. "You don't even know if he wears a white hat."

"But I'm a damsel in distress and even if he's Black Bart, I think I'd like for him to rescue me," she said.

"You couldn't have chosen a better champion, my dear," said Kasia.

"See there, Stan. I do have a sense about these things," Monica said. "What's his name, Kasia?"

"Jack MacKenzie," Kasia answered, a smile tugging at her lips.

"Monica Michelle MacKenzie. It does have a ring to it!"

"Pastor Jack is now the leader of the castle chapel that Frederic has re-established at Domani z Camin," said Kasia.

"Bummer. And just when I had a new lease on my future. I'm afraid my sins will come between us," Monica sighed.

Everyone got out of their trucks and stood in a group as the man rode into their midst. Frederic made introductions, but it was plain to see that the rider had a message.

"Count Zurowski?" asked the young man, directing his words to Stefan.

"Yes. What news?" asked Stefan.

"A man arrived at the castle at dawn this morning, and he says he's an ambassador from his Fuhrẹr. The windows are tinted black, and his car flies a swastika on the antenna, and he wears the red armband like the one you're wearing with Hitler's signature." His voice was low and melodic. "Our people at the castle disappeared immediately when they saw the car, and I haven't seen them since."

"I'll explain later, but does he have a small boy with him?" asked Stefan.

"I didn't see one. But he did say that he had a package to give to you when you reached the castle. Are you expecting him?" asked Jack.

"Oh, yeah. He's holding our son hostage," Stefan growled. "That 'package' is my little boy. I have something he wants very badly."

"Do you want to borrow my horse and leave your trucks here?" Jack offered. "But as far as I've been able to tell, there's only one official car driven by one Nazi officer. He doesn't even have a driver. Domani z Camin has been left alone for several months, and this man doesn't seem to be posing a threat. Just waiting."

"Thanks, it might be safer to leave all of our cargo here." Stefan turned to those around him. "Stay here until you see the

German car drive away. We can't afford to take chances on an ambush."

Sophia started to protest, but Stefan held her close for a moment before he mounted the horse. "Trust me," he whispered.

Stefan rode quickly but slowed the horse to a trot as he crossed the drawbridge to the castle. The sound of the horse's hoofs vibrated in time to his heavy heartbeat echoing in his ears. His mouth felt dry.

When he reached the castle door, a man in a uniform sporting a red arm band on his black sleeve, stepped out. He offered a Sieg Heil salute, "Heil Hitler!"

Stefan ignored the greeting. "I'm Count Zurowski. I believe you have a package for me?"

"No greeting, Count?" His mustache caused his upper lip to disappear when he sneered, allowing his upper teeth to look threatening.

"Good morning. Let's get on with our trade," said Stefan.

"Yes, my Fuhrer is very anxious for this trade. I have the honor of being his special envoy sent on delicate missions such as this. My name is Wilhelm Stendal, and I have the distinction of being with the Fuhrer's personal working staff. Do you have the package?" he asked. Stefan could see why this man would be sent. His round, ruddy face oozed innocence, a threat to no one.

"And do you have yours?" Stefan demanded.

"Of course. Follow me," he moved smartly to his car. The car windows were completely darkened, allowing nothing inside to be seen.

He opened the car door and stepped away so that Stefan could see that Konrad was tied up in the back seat. He appeared to be asleep.

Stefan knelt down to feel the boy's pulse and felt his forehead, "If you've hurt him…"

"The boy isn't harmed, but he was easier to transport asleep. Seems he has a fighting spirit," Stendal taunted. "Now, let's see your package."

Kasia had removed the stitches to the secret hiding place in Stefan's coat the night before, and he had the velvet-lined box containing the crucifix tucked into the waistband of his trousers under his coat. He pulled it out.

"Here it is," said Stefan, handing it to the shorter man.

Stendal took the box and opened it, revealing the crucifix. The noonday sun caught the precious stones and they glowed as if electrified. The light shining from his eyes was nearly maniacal. It was evident that he shared his Fuhrer's belief in the occult.

"Ah, yes, this will make a difference," he whispered under his breath. He stowed it in a small case and locked it. "Take your son," he instructed.

"This kidnapping was not part of the deal. I don't know if this coercion from your side will affect the transfer of prosperity to the new owners or not. The curse is an unknown entity. If an evil burden does fall on unworthy persons, it is unknown if its return to the previous owner will lift the torment." Stefan hoped that he was playing to this man's superstitions because he was making up his words as he went.

"Don't try to threaten me, Count," said Stendal. He was clutching the box to his chest, walking quickly back to his car.

As soon as Stefan had taken Konrad from the car, the German officer drove off.

The trucks then started to the castle. It was slow going because of the poor condition of the narrow, potholed road.

"Job number one for the bulldozer," stuttered Ish as his seat bounced and he hit his head on the roof above.

Chapter 16

Stefan stood holding Konrad in his arms as he watched the vehicles drive through the courtyard, stopping just outside the bridge that spanned the moat. No other vehicles were in sight; so, perhaps, it was safe to let down their guard a little. They would need many things unloaded soon, but his first concern was his son.

Stefan carried the boy, and the others followed him, to the castle's entrance, up the wide stairs, and on into the large expansive hall. The tripartite edifice had housed Zurowskis for many decades, and they now stood in the palatial living area of the castle. Whether the family was large or small, there had always been bedchambers for all and unoccupied rooms and space to spare. Echoes from their footfalls were bringing life to the emptiness.

Dr. Janda jumped from the truck, hurrying toward Stefan. The others followed quickly, Sophia in the lead.

"Over here, Stan," said Stefan, "on this divan."

Stanislas took his stethoscope from his bag and opened the boy's coat. He pressed it to the small, bare chest. His brow furrowed.

"What's wrong?" Sophia's voice was forced.

"He's been given too many sedatives. Stanislas raised the sleeve of the boy's coat and added, "he has several needle marks on his arm. Too many sedatives can depress the central nervous system and cause unconsciousness, and I don't know what they've given him." He raised the child to a sitting position and listened to his lungs through his back. "His breathing is a bit erratic."

"What can you do?" Stefan and Sophia asked together.

"I'll start an IV and get him hydrated. This should help flush out the medication through his system. His vital signs are stable, and he should wake up soon. I'll want him monitored constantly and call me as soon as he wakes up."

"I'm a nurse. May I help?" asked Leah as she stepped forward. She had been silent since they left Warsaw.

"Thank you. I'm sure we can use your help." Stanislas had been watching Leah since she'd joined them. Her loveliness kept his attention, but there was something else. She'd eaten very little at their rest stops, and he was sure she was having bouts of nausea. He didn't know where she came from, but she needed rest, and it was impossible to get any in the back of that truck. His heart went out to her with feelings that were more than sympathy. He hated to ask anything from her now, but he would need experienced help.

Dr. Janda looked around at the vaulted ceilings and museum-like opulence and turned to Frederic. "Is there a room somewhere that can be set up as a clinic? "

"Of course, follow me," Frederic said.

"I'll need to stay with Konrad for a while; but if you show Leah the way, she can take some of the medical supplies and begin to set up. I know we have a patient still in the truck, too. Sarah wasn't able to walk in, and we'll need to start inoculations for those living on the estate as soon as it can be arranged. They probably haven't been able to be careful in what they ate or drank," said Stanislas. "Do you mind, Leah?"

"Of course not." She wouldn't meet his eyes. He might read her secret.

"Leah, if you'll wait here, Jack and I will get Sarah from the truck, and then I'll lead the way to the room you can use," Frederic said.

Jack and Frederic walked out of the great hall and out through the main entrance, and Jack carried Sarah back in.

Stanislas couldn't explain the sudden averseness he felt as he watched Monica's 'hunk of a cowboy' follow Leah out of his sight.

Frederic had anticipated the need for a place that could be used for a sick room and led the way to a room that had an entrance into the courtyard that would be easily accessible by the estate tenants. He had equipped it with four small cots, a cooler chest to accommodate medicines with an extra freezer box, and shelves for storing medical supplies. The wash-up sink was deep with a soap dispenser. Electrical outlets provided for sterilization paraphernalia, and ceiling-mounted lights and white walls provided for good visibility.

A sturdy rocking chair padded by thick cushions sat in a corner, possibly for one who was keeping a long-night's vigil. Sophia now sat in the chair holding Konrad, softly singing his favorite nursery song, and watching for a fluttering of his eyelids.

Nearby, Leah was expertly assembling the IV pole for gravity infusions.

Dr. Janda entered the room carrying the bags and looked around. "Frederic, I'm amazed. I don't think I've ever been in a better-equipped clinic."

"Jósef Zurowski instructed me to provide the best available for Domani z Camin. He told me to spare no expense," Frederic explained. "It did take a while to get the things here, but it happened."

"Indeed, it did!" Then Stanislas turned to Leah, "Excellent job, nurse. Are we ready to get Konrad juiced up?" He succeeded in getting an answering smile from the girl.

"I think this will be easier if Konrad is lying on the bed," Leah began, looking at Sophia, "do you mind placing him here?" She indicated the cot beside where the pole now stood.

Sophia carefully rested Konrad on the clean, white sheet and covered him with a light blanket and watched as Stanislas positioned the pole lower to reach his small patient. She flinched as she watched alcohol being rubbed on the skin and a small needle being inserted into a tiny vein on the back of the little hand. His hand had been cleaned, but traces of soil was deep under his fingernails. Where had his kidnappers kept him?

Sophia watched the liquid drip slowly into her young son who still showed no signs of consciousness. Hatred filled her, and she thought of her revolver snug in its holster at the bottom of her tote bag.

Chapter 17

Gradually, the tenants that had fled in isolation to the small town of Wegorzewo heard that Domani z Camin was again safe and began to sneak back under cover of darkness. The cottages that had been abandoned were again occupied. Many had not escaped the Russian soldiers' attack upon the estate, but the remaining family members were back to work the land.

Routines were established. Stefan was the reigning Count Zurowski, and as such, went from cottage to cottage, introducing Sophia, the new Countess, and welcoming them back. Some remembered the harshness of Stefan's father and displayed cautiousness in their greetings. Sophia's openness helped allay some of their misgivings.

Ish followed their visits, gathering information on the condition of their fields. It was of great concern since many of the oxen they'd used for plowing had been slaughtered for food. Ish instructed a few young men on the use of the new tractor they'd brought and appointed an overseer to see that each farm was cultivated to enable sowing. An up-front cash payment to each farmer would tide him and his family over until he could realize funds from a profitable crop.

Word went out that Domani z Camin would buy oxen, horses, cows, and goats to replenish their destroyed animals. Pasture fences were made secure and out-buildings repaired in preparation for new livestock. Farm machinery of all kinds was needed. Things that had been hidden when the threat of attack came, resurfaced, and was put to use.

Kasia and Manka visited each cottage giving staples that had been in short supply or even nonexistent. Bags of flour, sugar, shortening, coffee, and tea were added to the pantries of each household. Seeds were given that could be sprouted in makeshift greenhouses for transplanting into summer planting for their kitchen gardens. Those who'd been able to plant cool-weather crops shared their cabbages, onions, brussels sprouts, and beets with them. The farm women hungered for neighborly talk and shared recipes, fulfilling a need nothing else could touch. The excitement over receiving new bolts of cloth and skeins of yarn bubbled up over their hardships.

Woodshops were repaired, the blacksmith's forges rebuilt, leathermaking, and all the craftwork that it took to make Domani z Camin a self-sustaining entity again became workable.

Ish bulldozed the surrounding courtyard into submission and appointed gardeners to prepare the lawn and planting beds according to the layout he'd drawn for its reconstruction. Stone paths were laid, and many of the toppled statues and sculptures were located, repaired, and again gave definition to the landscape. The statues of twelve Teutonic Knights again stood upright along the path in the courtyard. Bricks were made from the red clay soil nearby and the walls again stood complete. The damaged bridge over the moat was reinforced with rock from the nearby limestone quarry, looking like Ish remembered it long ago.

Frederic had ordered the repair of most of the damage that had been within the castle. Paintings were still being restored and tapestries rewoven to complete the scenes that once told of past exploits, but the plans were being carried out. Ahead of the attack of the Russian soldiers in 1939, the old Count had stored much in the castle keep. Even the furniture had been relocated there, leaving only the bare necessities to keep the household going. Frederic was able to have the things returned to their original placement, welcoming Stefan back to the home he remembered before the damaging attack of the Germans. Kasia had supervised the repair and re-outfitting of the kitchen areas.

The castle on the estate of Domani z Camin was coming back to life.

Chapter 18

Konrad regained consciousness, but periods of lethargy left him uninterested in anything around him. He hadn't spoken as yet, but he started at loud noises and screamed if all the lights were out. When little Jan had babbled at him as he offered a toy, he looked at his brother as if he didn't know him. He did hold tightly to a Lego block from the set Monica had bought him before leaving New York.

Monica was sitting by the sleeping boy, rubbing the frown from his brow.

"Aunt Monkey?" The eyes were wide and the voice a whisper.

Monica wanted to run and tell them that Konrad was talking, but she sat still, afraid any quick movement would frighten him.

"Yep, it's me. Your Aunt Monkey," she gave a tremulous smile with her words.

"Aunt Monkey?" he said again, stretching out his hand.

Monica took his small hand and planted a kiss on its palm.

"What can I get you?"

"Stay with me. Don't let them put me in the dark." There was panic in his whisper.

"Count on me, kid. Aunt Monkey won't let anyone get you ever again," she said firmly.

"Do you have a gun?" he asks.

"Sure do," she answered.

"Ok," he said and closed his eyes. The frown was gone, and he slept peacefully still holding on to Monica's hand.

Monica pressed the call button on the bed, and Leah came into the room.

"Hi, Monica," she said, "how's he doing?"

"He woke up and talked to me. Will you please get Sophia? He asked me to stay with him."

Dr. Janda came into the room followed by Stefan and Sophia.

"He talked?" Stefan and Sophia asked together. They watched as Stanislas checked the boy's vital signs and nodded his head.

"Everything seems good," he assured them. "We'll have to find a stimulant for him. Something to hold his interest."

"His sleep looks peaceful for the first time," Leah added.

"We'll stay with him for a while, Monica," said Sophia. "You've been here all day."

Monica lifted the small hand she still held into Sophia's hand, explaining he didn't want to be left alone.

Monica felt dismissed. As soon as she closed the clinic door and was in the courtyard, she let the tears fall and ran down a flagstone path. He wasn't her child, and she'd let herself become too attached to him.

She rested on a stone bench, closed her eyes, and let the sun dry the tears on her cheeks.

"It's a beautiful day," a voice beside her said.

She quickly stood and started to leave.

"Don't go, I won't bite," his voice was warm and friendly. "You want to tell me, lass, what's caused the tears?" The Scottish brogue was her undoing and tears flowed again.

"No sympathy, please," she snapped, "I'm not used to it."

"Not even from your 'hunk of a cowboy'?" he asked.

'Oh, dear, who told you what I said?"

"It was Kasia. You need to know she tells all. Actually, I'm a Scottish Laird, which I'm sure is a come-down from a cowboy," his teasing tone continued. "Disappointed?"

"So, where's your Tam 'O Shanter? Your bagpipe?"

"At home in the Highlands, lass," his laughter was contagious. "Don't wear my Scottish Bonnet here."

Monica was captivated by his light, iris-colored eyes.

"Aye," she mimicked, "it would be a shame to cover up your blond locks. Traded in your Tartan Sash for a clerical collar?"

"Now, lass, don't downplay the tartan pattern of my clan. 'Tis a sacred thing in the Highlands."

"Okay, truce," she extended her hand. The larger hand that wrapped around hers was calloused from labor. "Tell me how you came to pastor this estate church?"

"Oh, nothing so grand as that. Sounds like Kasia is trying to make me important," he said. "I'm conducting Bible studies until the replacement pastor arrives."

"I'm still impressed. So, what happened to the former leader?" she asked.

There was a pause, and Monica wasn't sure he had heard her. He was gazing over her shoulder to the castle.

"My father was a missionary in Warsaw but left to pastor here. He and my mother were killed when the Russian soldiers first attacked Domani z Camin. Frederic notified me when it would be safe to try and get here, but I came and was able to give my parents a final memorial. It wasn't without some tense moments I can assure you."

"I'm sorry, Jack. I didn't know," Monica was sorry she'd opened the subject. *She guessed there were some things that even Kasia didn't feel free to tell.*

"When I came of age, father turned the family wool mill over to me. We do it all, from raising Scottish Dunface short-haired sheep to distributing the finished woolen products worldwide," Jack spoke with family pride. "But he had his heart set on missionary work and was just waiting until I could take over. He knew it was dangerous, but when the post in Warsaw became available, he felt called to take it."

"So, who's minding the store back in Scotland?"

"We have trustworthy sheepmen and expert weavers. We have managers in each of our stores throughout the United Kingdom. My older sister has a staff to handle marketing and filling orders. She tells me woolen orders from the makers of military uniforms are pouring in," he massaged his temple, "so I must get back as quickly as I can."

"Brothers?" she asked.

"One younger. But we can't get him out of the sheep pens," he laughed. "Enough of me. I haven't said this much since I've been in Poland," he closed the subject. "What caused your tears, lass?"

"Me? Monica? Tears?" she objected. "No way."

"Yes, you."

Chapter 19

They both sat in silence: Jack was waiting for Monica to respond, and Monica was struggling against the need to unburden herself. She tried to focus on the bees flitting from flower to flower, enjoying the fragrance and nectar in the newly-planted Corn Poppy border along the flagstone path. Ish had told her that this red poppy was the national flower of Poland.

"Konrad finally talked this morning," she began.

"That's good news?" he asked. "So, were those tears of joy? Relief?"

"Nothing so pure or unselfish I assure you," she mocked. "I was feeling sorry for myself. When I summoned the doctor and his parents to tell them, I was told they would stay with him now. I could take a rest. I was being shown the door, Jack."

"Didn't they ask what he said?"

"No, and he was asleep when they did come into the room. I didn't get a chance to tell them that he was afraid. He asked me not to leave him and if he wakes again, I'll not be there," she paused, "he can't say Monica, calls me 'Aunt Monkey'."

It was too much. Monica bent her head to her lap and sobbed. Gently, Jack pulled her up, positioned her head to his shoulder, and held her while she cried. Her sobs ended in hiccups, then stopped.

"I've not had any responsibility in the family and have been considered an outsider, but I'm important to little Konrad," she said.

"I'm sure he's not the only one," he said. "I sense compassion in you, and you were brave enough to come with the family to Domani z Camin in this dangerous time."

"Stefan was against bringing me," she said. "He told me I just couldn't call a taxi and return home."

Jack sensed the hurt she felt. "Perhaps he was protecting you."

"Maybe. But I feel like he thought I'd be in the way or starved for entertainment," her tone was resentful. "After my brother died, Jósef Zurowski allowed me to go to New York City. I explained to them that I only felt alive when surrounded by the bright lights of the big city. But the truth was that I had to get away from the accusation I thought I saw in Stefan's eyes."

"Do you wish to tell me what you were being accused of?" asked Jack.

"No, I don't want to, but I might as well. But I'll never be able to look at you again without feeling shame."

"Shame?' His brows lifted in surprise.

"The real Monica isn't a pretty sight, and…"

"From where I sit, the real Monica is quite a beautiful sight," he responded, as he brushed a strand of her black hair back from her face.

"Outwardly, maybe," she turned her face away. "My brother, Maurice, had certain, how shall we say, 'weaknesses'. He abused Sophia with unwanted attention from the time Jósef married our aunt until the time he died in an accident. I think Stefan thought I knew and should have alerted Jósef. I honestly didn't know; Maurice and I were never close."

"Seems like Sophia should have told someone," Jack reasoned.

"I certainly would have!" Her green eyes flashed. "But when I left Forest House, I'm sure they could erase all memory of my having been there. Stefan and Sophia had each other, Jósef had serious business decisions, and I was an 'extra'."

"What about Stanislas?" he asked. "Manka seems to think you were together."

"Not in this lifetime!" she denied. "We had fun, but he was more of a brother to me than my own brother. I certainly never aspired to be a doctor's wife. And I don't think he ever contemplated making me one." Their laughter blended.

"What were your interests?"

Monica looked at him. Suddenly, she was aware that this was the first time anyone had cared enough to ask what she wanted. Certainly, the first time any man had tried to get to really know her.

"When I first arrived in New York, I enrolled in a school for fashion design and did some modeling. I volunteered in a children's daycare that kept preschoolers of women working in factories for the war effort. And…"

"And?" he probed.

"Okay, I did do the nightclub scene! But I don't drink and I think that's what most of those with me had to do to have a good time," she said. "After a while, they didn't even want me around. I was left with only a few friends. Wet blanket, I suppose." Her sigh was accompanied by a self-deprecating shrug.

"Don't be so critical of yourself. I like all I've heard," he said. "I think you'll qualify for a position I have open."

"Yeah? Am I interested?" she asked, her eyes widen slightly. "And just why would you think I'd accept?"

"You like children."

"And? I'm still in the dark here," she stammered.

"I'm handling this clumsily," he started "but it's this. The village church has a preschool for the tenant children. The teacher is a little overwhelmed with the growing numbers now coming to class. She told me she needs a story lady."

"A story lady. You want me to be a story lady?" she nearly snorted.

"Why not? Pick a story. Read it to the kids. How hard can it be?"

"In Polish? I don't speak Polish," she exclaimed.

"No, the teacher is teaching them English," he said.

"I don't know…" she hesitated.

"It might be good for Konrad," he began, "give him something that might spark a little interest. His 'Aunt Monkey' as a story lady. Sounds perfect, and it would give you more time with him."

"It's not fair to use my nephew against me," she said. *It would be something useful that she could do. So far, no one had asked her to help with anything.* "I'm not sure they'd let me take Konrad out of the castle."

"Not even with your 'hunk of a cowboy' riding shotgun?" he teased.

"Not on your life. But if a Scottish Laird charged in, mounted on his mighty steed, brandishing his protective claymore, there might be a wee chance."

"Then we'll see what we can arrange."

She could still hear his laughter as she ran back up the path to the castle. There, she headed straight for the library. She would pick up the gauntlet he'd thrown, and she would give his challenge her best shot.

Chapter 20

The library at the castle was extensive, but Monica scanned the books until she found the one that suited her purpose, *Poland's Favorite Fairytales*. It was dog-eared, and she could just make out the childish scrawl that said 'Stefan Zurowski'. This would do; no use telling the fairytales from her childhood. Give the children something familiar. Clutching the book to her chest, she went to her room with thoughts of costumes in her head. If she was going to be a story lady, she'd look the part. She'd try out her costume and story on Konrad, and then she'd suggest they tell it to the younger kids at the school. Perhaps, she could help take away some of his fears.

A week later, she was ready.

"Aunt Monkey, is today the time to tell our story? Can I dress up in my costume?" Konrad bounced on his feet as his questions ran together.

"Today's the day. Jack will be here to drive us to school soon. Let's get ready!" Monica wasn't sure if her nervousness came from telling the story or being with Jack.

"I'm gonna be the thoe maker," lisped Konrad, "I'll be a hero! Wait for me. Don't go."

"Wouldn't leave you, Konrad," assured Monica, "now let your momma get you dressed while I turn into the 'story lady'."

"Aunt Monkey?" asked Konrad.

"What is it? You don't have to be afraid. Jack and I will be with you all the time," assured Monica.

"No, not that," he protested, "I'm getting braver, but the kids will be hungry. Can we take them something?" His mouth twisted sideways.

"Hungry?" Monica was puzzled.

"Yeth," he stood firmly, waiting for her answer.

"What if the story lady brings a large basket of apples?" Monica suggested.

"Yeth, yum." He turned and scurried out of the room.

Monica had found a green vintage ballgown in a chest in one of the storage rooms. Manka had been able to get the musty odor out, and Monica had trimmed the square neckline and billowy sleeves in a gold braid that Manka had given her from her sewing basket. There was also a long velvet cape with a hood, and a pearl-studded snood that would complete her costume.

"Monica, you look lovely," Sophia exclaimed. "That's your color! It matches your eyes."

"Thanks, Sophia. I find I need a confidence booster to meet with youngsters."

"You'll do great."

"How do I look?" Konrad pranced on his toes.

"Like a proper shoemaker," Monica said. Konrad's long-sleeved yellow shirt was tucked into blue cotton trousers that stopped at his ankles above short boots. His suspenders were black. He held a soft leather shoe in one hand, and a large-eyed threaded needle in the other. Jack carried the wire cage twisted to look like a sheep. It was covered with a white, wool blanket cut to fit the frame and stood on four wooden legs.

This was Monica's debut as story lady, and Konrad's first trip out of the castle since he awoke from his coma. He had been watching children play in the courtyard, so maybe this would give him the confidence to join them outside.

The Zurowski carriage delivered them in style. The children were silent as Monica, Jack, and Konrad took their places in chairs at the front.

As the children made their way to their chairs in a semi-circle around her, Monica saw what Konrad was trying to tell her. All of them were thin, and some of them probably were hungry. Their eyes followed the basket of apples as she placed it on the desk behind her.

Before taking his seat, Konrad took the basket of apples and let each child take one. The children cradled them in their hands and turned their eyes to Monica.

"My name is Miss Monica, and I've come to tell you a fairytale today. Konrad is my helper and when I say the word 'dragon', he will roar. But he will need for all of you to roar with him because it's a very, large dragon." She settled back and smiled at the eager faces turned to her.

"The name of my story is 'The Dragon of Krakow.' Once upon a time…," she paused, "that's how all the fairytales in my country begin."

"That's America," Konrad interrupted. "We came here on a big boat."

"Once upon a time," Monica continued, "there was a good king named Krak, and he had a very, large kingdom. He wanted to build a village in the very center of his land where a beautiful blue river flowed, where trees grew, and birds sang. The river would bring in trade, there would be dressmakers, shoemakers, bakers—all kinds of shops to make the village rich.

King Krak picked a site on top of a green, grassy hill to build his castle. He brought in his team of advisers to look over the land."

"It's beautiful," they said, "but there is only one thing wrong."

"What's that?" asked King Krak.

"Underneath the hill that your castle will be built upon is a cave. Inside the cave is a large, speckled egg as tall as me. It's been there for many years."

"That egg has been there so long it probably won't ever hatch," said the King, "let's build my castle."

"So, the builders got busy and built a big castle that covered the entire hilltop. It was beautiful, the town grew rich, and all the king's subjects were happy," read Monica.

"And then…" Konrad interrupted.

"Yes, and then, one night in the dark, a loud CRACK woke up everyone in the castle. The king sent messengers out with torches to see what made that loud noise."

"Well, what was it?" cried the king when they returned.

"A dragon," a messenger told him, "and he ate some of our men."

Konrad turned to the other children, and they all roared.

"The next morning the king looked out of his window and there was the dragon," Monica smiled as the children roared again.

"He was flying in the air, his tail so large that it nearly blocked out the sun, his head held such large teeth that he could've crushed the castle with one bite. He dived down to take a bath in the Vistula River, and the water flowed out of the banks down the village streets.

"The dragon grew and grew and became quite fat from eating so many cattle. When the dragon was in his lair, steam came up through cracks in the cave ceiling making the castle walls wet and slimy. He would hunt at night, eating sheep off of the meadows and picking cows right out of the barns. Flames coming out of his mouth burned the fruit orchards, and the ashes from the burning trees turned the Vistula River black.

The children were so caught up in the story that they forgot to roar.

"The dragon must be stopped," the king decreed. "Bring in my army of knights."

"Fearlessly the knights put on their armor, mounted their mighty steeds, and rode to face the dragon," Monica paused for another shout from the children. "But they couldn't slay the dragon. The dragon melted the armor with his hot breath, and he devoured the knights and the horses.

"The king sent his messengers out into the city to tell the citizens that they would be given whatever prize they wished if they could kill the dragon.

"One villager had a plan. It was the shoemaker," Monica pointed to Konrad who held up the shoe in his hand.

"He found a sheep's skin and cleaned it until it was white. He fluffed up its wool so that the dragon would think it was alive. He stuffed it with bags of sulphur inside the fake sheep.

Konrad stood and bowed, holding up his needle and thread. He gently rubbed the wool that covered the sheep-like structure, pretending to sew the sides together.

"The shoemaker traveled to a quarry outside the city and dug sulphur from the ground, filling several bags with the spicy, yellow grit which he stuffed inside the pretend sheep. He then placed the make-believe sheep in the pasture in plain sight just outside the cave entrance.

"Everyone hid behind trees where they could see the cave and waited and waited. And what do you suppose happened?

"Night came, and the dragon crept from the cave and spied the one lone sheep put there by the shoemaker. Flying up, and then down, the dragon opened his enormous mouth, and he swallowed the sheep, chomping down with his yellow, sharp teeth. The sulphur burned hot and spicy in the belly of the dragon and his tail swished everything away in its path. He rushed to the river and began to gulp, gulp, gulp so much water that the river became clear again. Gulp, gulp, more water, and his green scaly skin stretched him so tight he looked like a giant balloon. Gulp, gulp, more water until his skin burst open. The explosion was so loud that it was heard for a mile and the dragon's flame lit up the sky like fireworks. Pieces of the dragon flew everywhere. The shoemaker was a hero."

Konrad raised both arms in the air, smiling shyly at his new-found friends.

"Shoemaker, what can I give you for a reward for killing the Dragon of Krakow?" asked the king.

"May I have the skin of the dragon?" he asked. "I am a poor man, but I love making shoes. I know how it feels to walk on rocks, ice, and snow without any shoes. With the dragon's skin I can make lots of shoes for the poor."

"Your request is granted. And you shall have a new shoe shop built near the castle. And I hope that you have more shoes to make than there are feet in my kingdom."

Konrad held up his apple and took a big bite. Crunching sounds filled the small room as the children bit into their treats.

Chapter 21

"I think we'd better post guards on the grounds surrounding Domani z Camin," said Stefan as he and Stanislas were listening to news that Jack brought.

"He wasn't dressed as a soldier and had no visible weapons, but his mannerisms were hard to disguise. He asked, specifically, about any young women that might have shown up here," said Jack. "He said he'd volunteered to help her family search for her."

"That may have been just a way to ferret out other information," Stanislas said.

"He did describe her," Jack hesitated, looking at Stanislas.

"What did he say?" Stan asked, a suspicion wanting to surface.

"He said she was blonde and very fair, a true Aryan," Jack said.

"That sure gave him away as a German," said Stanislas.

"If he comes back, you can tell him we've not taken in any runaways," Stefan said. "But we've been granted immunity with no restrictions on whom we can shelter here on the estate. It's been several months now with no trouble.

"It could be someone trying to keep a path open to Konrad. If things start to take a downturn for the Nazi army, the supposed curse from the Jeweled Crucifix may be blamed. In his madness, Hitler may even order the death of Konrad," Stefan said. He bit on his lower lip anxiously.

"Why not just return the crucifix?" asked Jack.

"That would be too easy. I don't think we can expect sound judgment from their Fuhrer. His occult dabbling has turned into rabid belief. Ownership of the Zurowski Jeweled Crucifix is supposed to solidify his ultimate victory," said Stefan.

"I'll go tell Ish that we need to set up guards," Stefan said as he turned to leave. "And ask around to see if anyone else has been approached by someone asking questions."

Jack and Stanislas watched him leave them to find Ish.

"You thinking what I'm thinking?" asked Jack.

"Maybe," Stanislas said hesitantly.

"If it's true, we'll have to find a way to protect her," Jack said. "I wonder why Stefan never thought of it?"

"Stefan has the heavy responsibility of rebuilding Domani z Camin," said Stanislas, "and he only has eyes for his red-haired wife."

"She is a looker but not the one I had in mind," Jack said. "Nor is it the bonnie lass with green eyes and black hair."

"So, you've noticed Monica, huh?"

"Noticed her? She's impossible to miss," Jack admitted.

"You have to be tough to take on Monica," Stanislas said.

"I think I may take on that assignment," Jack offered, smiled, then continued. "But we know the stranger isn't looking for Sophia or Monica."

"No, I agree, it must be Leah," Stanislas sighed, heavily. "She's an efficient nurse. I speak little Polish and without her I wouldn't know what many of the patients are saying. But even with her excellent medical skills, she's much more adept keeping her personal life hidden."

"Ish thinks she's his brother David's daughter, but he's never talked to her. He plans a trip to Warsaw soon to start his search for his brother. David may not have survived; but if he's alive, Ish says he'll be with the resistance." Jack watched Stanislas look off toward the door to the clinic. "And she's never said a word as to where she's come from?"

"No, Jack, it's frustrating to work with someone so closely and know nothing about them. I guess I'll have to bring up the subject now that it seems it might cause trouble here on the estate."

Leah gathered supplies to restock the shelves in the clinic. It was surprising how much had been accomplished. The typhoid vaccinations had been administered to all the tenants along with the vaccinations to the children against childhood diseases. With the growing number of people now working the farms, there were accidents requiring stitches and splints along with snake bites and summer colds. The days were a whirlwind of activity, and she could put her mind at rest as they kept busy in the clinic.

She had watched as the bulldozer went back and forth, back and forth, smoothing the ground, preparing a smooth surface. Dr. Janda, *he told her to call him Stan,* said yesterday that the runway was now finished, and a plane from America was expected soon. Besides things ordered by those living in the castle, there would be necessities for the farms and more new medical equipment, medicines, and supplies for the clinic. Their facility was already better furnished than any place she'd ever worked before.

She hadn't eaten so well since things were normal before the war started. That seemed so far in the past. Kasia and Manka prepared supper every night where they all gathered together as a family. She listened as everyone talked of the events of the day. She was grateful just to listen and briefly answer any questions that came her way about her day at the clinic. Breakfast and lunch were prepared and left on a table to fit into each one's individual schedule.

As she continued stacking laundered sheets in a small closet, she heard the outer clinic door open and shut. When she reached the waiting room, she saw that it was Stan who'd entered. She was puzzled as he locked the door.

"Leah, we have to talk," he said, as he motioned for them to enter his office.

"Sure," she replied slowly. The nausea in her stomach threatened to embarrass her.

"Have a seat," he pointed to the loveseat against the wall, and he took the armchair facing her. He ran his hand quickly through his thick, brown hair.

"What is it, Stan?" she asked. The expression in his brown eyes gave nothing away.

"A man came to Domani z Camin asking questions. Stefan is convinced it's a spy checking on the whereabouts of Konrad in case something goes wrong with the crucifix exchange," began Stanislas.

"They do keep a close watch on the child," Leah squirmed uneasily in her seat.

"Leah, you know you can trust me, don't you?" he asked.

"Yes," she said hesitantly, "why do you ask?"

"The man asked specifically about a runaway girl: a blonde-haired, blue-eyed girl with fair skin. Whom do you think he meant?" Stan continued to look at her, but she didn't answer his question.

"I think he was asking about you, Leah," said Stan.

"What did he look like?" Leah finally acknowledged him.

"Jack was the one who saw him and talked with him. He said he was a young man in civilian clothes with the mannerisms of a German soldier. He had a slender build, light-brown hair; and, oh, I think Jack said he had a scar on the right side of his face that puckered a line from his ear to his chin."

"I'll leave. I was looking for a place to hide, and I'd heard that Domani z Camin was abandoned; I was on my way here when I happened to find Sarah, and your caravan took us in. I don't want to repay the kindness I've received by putting everyone in danger."

"You can't leave. I need you here," Stan said. He couldn't account for the panic he felt at never seeing her again.

"It won't be long before no one will want me here," she turned her face away from him.

"You mean the baby?"

"How do you know?" she asked, quickly. "Does everyone know?"

"I don't think anyone is suspicious, but I'm a doctor, Leah. The signs have been plain enough. Especially working side by side all these weeks."

"I've been careful. You must have been watching me closely," she retorted.

"You aren't hard to look at," Stan watched her cheeks turn pink.

She wished she could control her emotions, but her face always gave her away. She'd hid her bouts of nausea as well as she could, but she was afraid at times he had been aware of why she would quickly leave the room. She knew her height would help when it became necessary to hide an expanding waistline.

"I'll pack and leave first thing in the morning. I don't want to put anyone here in danger," she said. "Besides, I couldn't bear them looking at me with disdain or pity."

"You misjudge these people, Leah. They've all had their sorrows," he defended. "What about the baby's father? Does he know?"

"I'm not sure, but you don't understand. I know the young man who came to Domani z Camin today. I recognized the description of the scar. The baby's father sent him out scouting for me," desperation tinted her voice. "I must leave here."

"Go where?" Stan asked.

"I don't know," she said, forcefully. "But he won't give up."

"Tell me, Leah," Stan urged. "We will figure out something."

"I'll tell you only so you can see how hopeless it is," she sighed in surrender.

"I was in Jedwabne visiting with my father when the slaughter began," her eyes went toward the window as though it framed the memories she was resurrecting. "The leader of the German soldiers was Bruno Stroop. When the Germans left, Bruno said he took me as his battle trophy; the Polish townspeople finished killing all the remaining Jews," bitterness made her words difficult. "I fought him as hard as I could, but he said he saw my father run off into the woods, and he wouldn't sound the alarm if I would go with him quietly."

"But you don't look Jewish," Stan said.

"There's no physical description that marks someone as a Jew," she retorted.

"Sorry. I'm just surprised. You look like a Viking princess," Stan's face reddened at his own words.

"I did fight him like a Viking warrior throughout all the months that I was forced to live with him at the military camp," she added, "but he protested that he loved me and would take me back home with him. My coloring wouldn't raise any flags he said, and no one would dare question him."

'How did you get away?" Stan asked the question burning in his mind.

"I watched for chances to escape all the time. But when I had a hint that I might be carrying his child, I became desperate. I knew if he found out, he would never let me go."

"So, he didn't know?"

"I think he must have known. Late one evening a group of Polish resistance fighters attacked the camp."

"Was this the first time?" asked Stan.

"No, there had been other times; but this time the fighters were equipped with better weapons and this attack was quite effective. The attackers weren't strong enough against the German's superior weapons, but it gave me the time I needed to slip away from our quarters without being seen. I had a few things in a cloth bag in case I ever got a chance to escape; so, I added what food I found available and stuffed it in the bag. My only driving need was to get as far from the camp as possible."

"Maybe he'll think you perished," Stan said.

"He won't stop unless he finds my body. The compound was all noise and smoke, but through the din, I could hear him calling my name," she remembered, the memory ugly on her mind.

The two of them sat in silence, each shrouded with an uncertain present. No words were spoken as they contemplated their individual futures. She had to leave, and Stan had to let her go.

Stan knew of the massacre of Jedwabne. Ish had anguished over the news because the last letter he'd received from his brother had come from there. It was the event that had cemented Ish Jacobson's decision to make the trip on the *Baltic Queen* to Poland. He knew Ish and Manka decided to marry because there was a possibility that if he found his brother, he'd not return to Dark Forest.

"Marry me, Leah," Stan looked directly at her.

The glass tube she'd been holding in her hand dropped to the floor, shattering into splinters.

"Marry you? Why?" she stammered, as she stooped to gather the shards of glass.

"We need you here. You have nowhere to go, and the baby needs a name," Stan stated. "You weren't married to this German officer, were you?"

Anger reddened her face, "Of course not. I was just a convenience!"

"It sounds like he considered you more than that."

"That made it even more distasteful," she whispered.

"Marry me, Leah," Stan repeated.

"Are you really this altruistic," asked Leah "to take on damaged goods and a Nazi baby?" Her blue eyes iced over.

"I never thought of myself as that selfless, and the baby won't be born with a swastika tattoo on its arm." He didn't flinch at her words. He hadn't expected her to fall into his arms with gratefulness.

"What of the people here? Stefan, Sophia and the rest?"

"I've been teased about all the time and attention I've given you, so they won't be surprised," he hoped that would be true. Jack had ribbed him endlessly.

"So, you would want them to think the baby was yours?" she asked, incredulously. "Wouldn't they be suspicious?"

"If they were, they wouldn't say anything. They would be glad for us. There isn't much happiness in this war-torn country right now."

"But I don't love you," she stated simply.

"You will in time," he smiled. "My mother says I'm quite loveable."

"And, what about your parents?" She rubbed her hands together.

"They'll welcome you with open arms and spoil the child shamelessly."

"But how will this help if Bruno's spy comes back and keeps asking around. Someone will remember the blonde nurse at the clinic, and that's all he'll need to convince him of my whereabouts. It won't work," she said.

"Trust me. For now, let's prepare a future for you and the baby," he hoped his words comforted her. "I'll arrange it if you'll agree to marry me." *He knew his plan would require moving Leah away from* Domani z Camin *and out of Bruno Stroop's reach. He hadn't told her that part of his plan yet. One step at a time.*

"If you are sure, then I will marry you for the sake of the baby," she agreed.

"I'll make arrangements," he said over his shoulder as he left her standing alone in the clinic.

Stanislas went to Ish and told him he'd asked Leah to marry him.

"She's your niece, so I'll want your blessing," Stan said.

"I can't think of a better man," Ish slapped Stan on the back. "If you need my permission, you have it. Blessings on you both."

The ceremony was simple. The priest that had come from Danzig with Ish performed the marriage in the estate chapel. Monica insisted on making Leah a dress, and Manka and Kasia prepared a wedding feast for the reception held in the castle's Great Hall. It was a bright spot in the arduous task of getting the estate in order, relieving some of the stress from the day-to-day routine. No suspicions or incriminations were directed toward the couple.

The bride and groom were given a large bedroom with a sitting area and an adjoining dressing room. Stanislas slept on the single bed in that dressing room. He could watch over his Viking princess from here, and he knew it wouldn't always be this way.

Doctor and nurse went back to the clinic the next day to care for the endless line of patients that needed their attention. Hearing of their marriage, many of those who visited the clinic wished the doctor 'trzymam kciuki'. Leah told him it was a wish for good fortune. They were accepted.

Leah felt a burden had been lifted from her shoulders, but she couldn't tell if Stan was sorry or not that he'd entered into such a one-sided deal.

Chapter 22

Snow lay deep and the wind whirled, piling drifts along all the walls, sculptures appearing where there had been none. The bridge across the moat held the snow tightly within its walls. Silver light from the moon bounced smoothly off of every ice-encrusted object, and bare skeletal fingers thrust through the drifts to emerge as limbs set free from their colorless graves.

It was only six weeks before Christmas and plans were being made for the first Christmas celebration at Domani z Camin in several years. The kitchens would soon be filled with the smell of spicy goodness. The plane had arrived with barrels containing foodstuffs to restock the kitchen with things not yet available. Baskets were being filled with tins of food and spices as Christmas gifts to the tenants; last-minute baked goods would be added to supplement their holiday menus. Additional bolts of material had also been ordered along with skeins of yarn, embroidery thread and sewing necessities to be included with their gifts. Many of the families still weren't properly clothed and exposure to the winter was causing illnesses.

With the new equipment and fresh seeds that came over on the *Baltic Queen* in the spring, the farms had produced rye, wheat, barley, and oats enough for their needs. Their major crops of potatoes, sugar beets, and tobacco were productive enough for themselves and the overflow could be sold in the outlying villages. Their vegetable gardens provided daily supplies of tomatoes, cucumbers, onions, lettuce, peppers, cauliflower, and cabbage plus enough to store for the winter months ahead. Fish abounded in the many lakes, and ice fishing had warded off starvation many times.

Ish had overseen the pruning and replanting of the fruit orchards of sour cherries, plums, apples, pears, and hazelnuts as soon as he arrived at Domani z Camin. There was an adequate amount of fruit with the promise of next year's abundance. Bushes of raspberries and blueberries had been trimmed into submission. Strawberries were in rows covered with a protection of straw. Quantities of the dried fruit and nuts had been purchased from the tenants and stored in the castle pantries.

Not only was Domani z Camin occupied, but it was stretching and coming alive. Life in the castle was awakening growth in the surrounding acres. Yet, there was land still to be reclaimed and prepared to be useful. More grazing land would be needed to feed the new crop of calves expected in the coming spring.

Stefan had been able to locate and purchase good breeding stock; herds were increasing in quality as well as in number, and many cows were producing rich milk for cheese and butter. Beef cattle, pigs, chickens, and goats were flourishing, dispelling the fear of hunger that had plagued them for the past few years. Neighbor traded with neighbor what they had for what they needed.

It was a long task restoring the various castle wings for the family members residences. Likewise, the refurbishing of the work areas, baking tower, butteries, icehouse, and large kitchen areas.

Extra effort was made to hire the estate's older women who were knowledgeable of its former condition. They came when the sun was full up but hurried away with the first hint of twilight. Kasia had to explain the persistent superstition that since the Count and his family were killed and no one had been there to cover the mirrors, the departed souls may have entered them. Those who died would then spend eternity haunting the living as terrifying reflections, caught forever in the sheets of glass. Unexpectedly, most of the mirrors had escaped the violence of the attacking soldiers.

As night was approaching, the wind whirled around the castle, rattling the nearby trees against the windows, as if demanding entrance. The boys were safely tucked abed in the nursery with Sarah sleeping on a cot nearby. Stefan, Sophia, Stanislas, Leah, Ish, Manka, Frederic, and Kasia were gathered around the supper table in their nightly routine. As usual, Jack claimed the chair beside Monica. Each one offered their versions of the day's news and activities.

A hearty beef stew accompanied by fresh-baked rye bread and cheese acted as a defense against the cold. Dessert was paczki, pieces of dough filled with wild rose petal jam harvested from the estate grounds. These deep-fried pastries rounded out a simple evening meal.

Supper was now finished, and two young kitchen maids were standing by to remove the dishes and prepare for morning.

The family retired to the spacious room adjoining the dining room. The walls were heavily draped for warmth and displayed scenes of hunting expeditions in greens, browns, and burgundies. Many couches and upholstered chairs were fronted by coffee tables, game tables, and tables that held decorative lamps. A black, wrought-iron screen covered the wide mouth of the fireplace, the blaze roaring. A grand piano sat to the side, and many nights Sophia entertained them with Chopin waltzes and pieces of other favorite Polish composers.

A carving in the limestone wall above the fireplace depicted the ancient Wawel dragon of Poland, standing erect and spewing fire at those who dared defy him. When Stefan and his brother were youngsters, they pretended a dragon lived under their castle like the one that lived under the Wawel Castle in Krakow. They filled the village children with their stories of the strange roaring they heard at night coming from the depths of the castle.

"So, Ish, when do you plan to leave?" asked Stefan. The conversations around him stopped as everyone wanted to hear the response.

"With the onset of winter, I can be spared here," he began, "so I see no reason to wait any longer for my trip back to Warsaw."

"I agree," said Stefan. "You've finished the work you came to do."

It was silent. Domani z Camin meant sanctuary, and one of their number was about to venture back into the reality that they had been able to push away. Now it came to the forefront.

"Yes. Since 1940 when the Germans decreed the establishment of the Warsaw Ghetto, we know thousands of Jews died each month due to extreme overcrowding, too little food, and the disease and death brought on by unsanitary conditions. Just this fall, the surviving Polish rebels were forced into surrender," Ish's face twisted in anger.

"The final destruction and deportation of the Jews in the Ghetto was begun in May of '43. When they fought back with their meager weapons, Warsaw was razed just this fall of '44," Stefan added.

Tears ran down Leah's face as she listened. As a sob escaped her, Ish pulled her close and she clung to him.

"Leah," he began, gently, "I do believe that you are my niece. And if my brother, your father, is alive I will find him. Do you know anything of him?" Manka sat close to Ish, giving of her strength. The others turned to Leah, not wanting to miss her answer.

"I was visiting him in Jedwabne when the slaughter started. He called for me to run, and I did. I saw him elude the soldiers and run into the surrounding woods, going in the opposite direction, trying to draw attention away from me," Leah's voice was hoarse. "I do feel that he's alive."

Leah looked at Stanislas. She would not tell her story of kidnap, rape, and escape. She'd come to care for Stan too much to open her past to the others. He'd been kind to her and patient, and she wouldn't expose her secret before his friends. The baby she carried belonged to Stanislas in every way that counted. Everyone had accepted that fact. She'd given the baby to him, but she still withheld herself. Her reluctance was fed by her shame, and her guilt taunted that she could have fought her German captor more.

"Leah, I do think my brother is alive," Ish offered, taking Manka's hand to accept the comfort she was offering. "If there is anyone left fighting, David will be standing there beside them to the end."

"You don't think there's a chance that he might be in a concentration camp?" asked Jack.

"No way. He would fight anyone to the death that would try to force him onto a train that he knew was heading in that direction," Ish's voice brooked no opposition.

"Yes, father was like that." Leah leaned her back closer into Stanislas's chest.

"So, you've made your plans to return to Warsaw now?" asked Stefan. "We've been totally cut off from Warsaw and the outside, so I don't know how safe you'll be. But the red armbands may allow you to move around without being stopped."

"Well...," began Ish, "I did get some word." His words came out reluctantly. "The farmer that delivered the last breeding stock that you bought had been in Warsaw. He reported that all Jews, at least those that they could round up, had been shipped to camps. The Warsaw Ghetto is annihilated." The enormity of this announcement sounded like a death knell.

"I'll go with you, Ish," said Frederic. "Several months ago, I obtained a new pastor for our church, and I must find out if he is still able to come." He turned to Jack, "you've been patiently waiting for your parent's replacements, but I know you must return to your business."

"Aye, soon," agreed Jack. He felt Monica's eyes on him. He didn't look her way.

"We need a doctor and a nurse, too," Stanislas added. "In a few months, I'll be taking my family home." He'd never mentioned where they would make their home, and he felt her stiffen and pull up slightly. But he hoped that Leah would accept the fact that the only way he could keep her safe from the German officer was to take her out of the country. The young man with all the questions had been spotted every week as close to the estate as he could get before being turned away. Their red armbands still gave the guards immunity.

Much lay beneath the words that had been spoken. Silence enveloped the group as each tried to assess what the near future would mean for them.

"Sounds like the trip must be made," said Stefan, breaking the silence. "I guess the decision will be just who must make this trip."

"I'll go with Ish," said Frederic. "I'm known by many."

"And, I'll go," Jack said, quickly leaving the room without even glancing at Monica.

The storm still raging outside was forgotten by the tumult now swirling within each one inside.

Chapter 23

David Jacobson had watched as Warsaw lay in flames, crumbling. He knew in the last six years each civilian had had to become a soldier, fighting valiantly against the tribe of ubermenschen, those believing they were the ideal superior man of the future who could rise above conventional Christian morality to create and impose his own values.

After he'd made certain that his daughter disappeared into the wood as the massacre in Jedwabne began, he himself escaped through the trees. He could only pray that she would find safety.

He'd made his way to join the resistance fighters. He'd helped create new ways to sneak necessities given by Poles living outside to those forced to live inside the Ghetto. Jews and others considered undesirable were crammed inside, suffering daily from the lack of water, light, and food that was withheld by their captors. He'd seen the bodies of those who'd perished from starvation and disease litter the hallways of the buildings before being dumped outside in the streets.

Their weapons had been barricades, guns and ammunition smuggled into the Ghetto through the sewers along with handmade grenades, bottles filled with petrol that they wrapped in paper and threw at German tanks. David had seen engineers, professors, and craftsmen combine their ingenuity to provide electricity in the Warsaw Ghetto for a few, precious weeks. Wells had to be dug when the water supplies were cut off. People continued to buy and sell within their confines as long as goods were available. But the need was too great.

David knew that the source of power in the city's inhabitants rested in their solidarity and mutual devotion to the ideal of a free Warsaw. The German invaders endeavored to break this spirit but could not. Warsaw's brave citizens were the last to surrender in Poland, and this was only a pretend one.

After the last rebellion by the heroes living in the Ghetto, the German Army rolled over the remains of the Warsaw Ghetto, leaving it a vast, empty desert. That had been April 19, 1943, nearly seven months ago. The Jews that had been able to flee the German roundup needed places to hide. And he'd led them to designated safe houses, but many could only find shelter in caves outside Warsaw. Whether safe house or cave, provisions were limited. Those who were able-bodied fled as far from Warsaw as they could.

Now, David Jacobson was hidden in a shuttered house, tucked safely in the medieval part of Warsaw with a marketplace and narrow streets. This old section would not surrender, and to him it became a symbol of the whole struggle of Warsaw.

"We've fought a good fight, and it's not over. We'll never give in," David Jacobson's voice was slightly above a whisper. His two companions sat nearby, both unkept and bearded.

"You've been a good leader, your turn to rest," the shorter man said, "we'll stand guard tonight. You've pulled guard duty two nights now."

"Guess it's my turn to rest," David tried to smile as he stumbled toward the cot. He was asleep before the guards could take their posts.

After the first part of the night passed, David began to toss and turn on the narrow cot. He tried to sit up, but the pounding in his head held him tight to the mattress. His throat was dry, his lips parched, and the throbbing in his leg vibrated up his spine.

He'd not mentioned his wound to his companions, because at first the shrapnel had only seemed like a flesh wound.

Snow lay deep on the ground, and his companions eased the fever in David's body with rags dipped in drifts and brought to his bedside. A few aspirin tablets were all that was left of their medical supplies, and they dispensed them to make them last as long as possible. David's last thoughts before unconsciousness enveloped him completely were of his daughter and his older brother, Ish,

The castle at Domani z Camin was nearly out of sight as the men forced their way toward Warsaw. The snowplow had been attached to the front of the truck with extra fuel stored in the back that they'd need in case there was none available where they were going.

Dr. Janda had prepared a medical bag for them to take along with instructions on the use of some of the drugs. Manka and Kasia had prepared and packed provisions for their journey. Some they could cook over a fire; some they could eat as they traveled without stopping. In this weather, fuel for their bodies would be as necessary as fuel to keep the vehicle running. Dehydration would be a silent enemy.

"My Jewish body doesn't rebel at all being cloaked in this Catholic garb," Ish said, as he again donned his woolen monk's robe and hood as his disguise. "And I look good in it!"

"Aye, that you do! Covers you up," said Jack. "It's almost enough to make me want to convert."

The parting from those back at the castle had been before dawn, but everyone was awake to see them off. They'd eaten as much as they could hold, knowing that would probably be the last warm food for the day.

Jack had managed to see Monica alone, and he had held her close. "Keep the heid!" he'd whispered.

"And that means?" her lip trembled.

"Stay calm, don't get upset."

"Just come back." She kissed him hard and ran out before the others entered the room.

The wind from the night before had died down, but the cold was bitter and the drifts made it hard to define the road's edges. The terrain was flat in this area, removing any danger of sliding down a hill. The winch on their truck would be enough if they slipped into a ditch. Mostly, the ground was hard, frozen deep.

The trek to Warsaw was slow. The wind began again to beat the descending snow against the windshield, drowning out any words that might be spoken. Night was falling and the oncoming twilight and snow made visibility nearly impossible.

Jack was driving, and he turned to Frederic and shouted, "Shall we pull off? Would it be safe?"

"I know this road and there is a deserted cabin not too far off of it. Maybe we should try for it until this storm passes," he answered. "Let's park in that clearing on the edge of those trees yonder. The field is as hard as the road we're on. I know where we are."

Jack agreed. Ish and Frederic were much older than he, and that is one reason he'd volunteered to come. In case of trouble, they might need him.

The men donned their snowshoes, shouldered their backpacks, and pointed their flashlights into the woods. Frederic led the way and soon they spotted the cabin he'd expected.

"Did you see a light?" asked Ish.

"I did think I saw a flicker, like from a candle or lantern," answered Frederic.

They neared the cabin slowly, the crunch in the snow from their boots alerting any occupants to their approach.

"Sześć," Frederic called out in Polish. "Czy ktoś jest w domu?"

"Tak," the reply was timid. "Czy mogę ci pomóc?"

"We need a place to stay for the night. We can pay," Frederic had slipped into English.

The door opened to allow them in and was quickly shut behind them. The light they'd seen was from a flickering fire in the fireplace, threatening to go out.

"We're on our way to Warsaw and we're caught in this storm," Frederic explained.

Three members of the family huddled in a corner while the man talked to them.

"You are welcome here," the man's voice still held reluctance.

"We will pay. And we've brought our own food which we'll gladly share with you," Frederic offered. The man's frame was wide, but lack of nourishment had left him gaunt.

"My name is Antoni Kaminski, my wife, Lena, and our son Szymn. We don't own this cabin, and we've only been here a short time."

"Dziękuję Ci," responded Frederic. "Do you have more firewood?"

"I was only able to cut this small amount," the man apologized.

"If you'll show me the axe, I'll get us more," Jack stepped forward.

The man cowered a little before the rugged Scotsman but stood his ground. "Over by the back door." He pointed behind him.

Jack picked up the axe, stepped out into the night, and turned on his flashlight. With any luck, he'd find a dry tree sheltered against the back of the cabin.

A hook hung from a chain in the middle of the fireplace. Beside the hearth was a black, iron kettle that was cold, so these people hadn't had a warm supper. Ish looked around and wondered what they had been eating. From his pack he selected a container of stew that Manka made for them. Knowing Manka's foresight, there was enough and to spare. He'd also brought in from their stash in the truck a large, crusty loaf of bread.

Szymn helped Jack bring in the wood and stack it neatly in the corner. It would be enough to keep the cabin warm throughout the night. He built a small, hot fire for Ish's pot, and before long the aroma of heating stew was tantalizing them all.

"Momma, is this a feast?" Szymn eyed the stew and bread.

"Son, I believe it's manna from heaven," she answered Szymn, her eyes glistening in the firelight.

"Like when Moses was leading our people?" Szymn's eyes widened.

Lena looked around at the men, "A rabbi held classes for the children in the Warsaw Ghetto telling how God helped the Israelites."

"Yes," said Jack, "just like that. Let's offer a prayer of thanks." As he said a short prayer, they all bowed their heads. Jack opened his eyes as he said 'amen' and saw Szymn peeking through his fingers at the stewpot.

"Dig in, boy, there's plenty for all," said Ish as he ladled stew into chipped, mismatched bowls from the cabinet and passed around bent spoons he'd found in the same cabinet. He'd seen only a half loaf of rye bread there that they were probably saving for their breakfast.

Ish made coffee and they sat in companionable silence. He had removed his monk's hood and cloak, soaking the warmth from the fire.

"May I ask your name?" Lena Kaminski asked, shyly. "We'd like to thank you each personally."

"Oh, Mrs. Kaminski," apologized Ish. "Please forgive me, I simply forgot my manners. This big Scotsman here is Jack

MacKensie. My other friend is Frederic Debrowski. My name is Ishmael Jacobson, but everyone just calls me Ish."

Antoni Kaminski had been sitting quietly listening to his son chat with the men. The food had enlivened the lad, and he suddenly felt inadequate. He hadn't been able to provide for them. *What had this man said? His name was Jacobson?*

"You said Jacobson?" Antoni asked.

"Ish Jacobson, yes," he answered.

"There's a man named Jacobson who has become almost a legend in the Warsaw Ghetto," began Antoni, "David Jacobson. He was able to help so many by slipping in and out of the Ghetto with aid for those inside. They nicknamed him the 'Fantasy Mist'; he's there, then he isn't. The Nazis put a price on his head."

Ish's voice caught in his throat, "David Jacobson?"

"Yes, that's the name. Could you know him?" asked Antoni.

"He's my younger brother. We're on our way to Warsaw now to find him. Do you know anything about where he might be?"

"The Warsaw Ghetto is totally empty now. I know that most from there were transported to concentration camps, but he helped those few who escaped the Nazi trains to places of safety."

"Did he help you?" Ish asked.

"No, I didn't see him personally, but the man who helped me told me that the 'Fantasy Mist' had sent him. They are careful about using his real name before they know you."

"Where did they tell you and your family to go?" asked Frederic.

When the man hesitated, Szymn shouted, "A castle. We're going to a castle."

"Szymn," scolded his father.

"Would that castle be located at Domani z Camin?" asked Frederic.

"Yes, Count Zurowski's land. We're told it's safe there." Fear swept over the man's face. "Is this not so? It could be just a trick."

"No trick," Frederic assured him. "That's where we came from."

Frederic had more to offer. "When you get there, tell the Count that Frederic Debrowski sent you, and he will find work for you. What was your occupation?"

"Horses. I trained horses, built handmade saddles, yoke for oxen, and anything leather. My wife, Lena, is a schoolteacher."

"We need a new teacher at our estate school, Lena," Jack said. Her answering smile was tremulous.

"The Count is building up the livestock on the estate, and he will introduce you to the proper overseer. Sounds like you'll both find employment. You'll be assigned a place to house your family," as Frederic talked, tears rolled down the man's cheeks.

"What can I say. How will I thank him?"

"Your good work is all the thanks needed. You'll only have to travel a full day to reach Domani z Camin. It isn't far now."

"About your brother," Antoni started, "you might look in the old section of Warsaw. I don't know where he'd be, but the people there would protect him. They've not surrendered, but since the German attack on Old Town, much lays in ruins. Gone are parks, museums, cathedrals…" He became silent.

"Thank you, Antoni," said Ish. "Goodnight, everyone."

Ish and Jack made a pallet on the floor and dropped off to sleep immediately. From his pallet on the floor, Frederic overheard the soft whispers of the couple across the cabin, planning for their tomorrow.

Chapter 24

The snowstorm had surrendered its fight. Glazed moonlight iced a path back to the edge of the trees and their truck, showing no other tracks but theirs. Frederic was now driving and he followed the remembered road until dawn. They'd only taken time to make coffee and now drank it in the truck with Manka's honeyed breakfast rolls. There had been enough stew left so that the Kaminski family wouldn't be forced to travel on empty bellies. When they arrived at the castle, Manka and Kasia would assess the condition of the family and make sure to have their living quarters stocked with food until they could again provide for themselves.

They took turns driving all through the day. Frederic pointed out the few landmarks that were visible.

"We'll be on the outskirts of Warsaw tonight. I suggest we camp in the woods and enter the city by daylight. The roads will probably be dangerous at night, impassable with all the destruction. We'll need to wear our red armbands and walk through as though we own the place," Ish said.

"Good plan," agreed Frederic.

"I cut extra firewood while I was cutting at the cabin and stacked it in the back of our truck, so we can have a warm supper," Jack said.

"An even better plan," agreed Frederic. "I'm hungry and I'm not nearly as large as you." Their laughter echoed through the truck, relieving some of the tension that was building up as they neared their destination.

Snow wasn't nearly as deep here and didn't cover the landscape. Frederic stood with the other two men and looked over the ruins. The Old Town was bounded by the Gdansk Boulevards along with the Vistula River, Grodska, Mostowa, and Podwale Streets.

"This has been done since we came through Warsaw!" Frederic stood in awe of the scene before them.

"There was news that the churches of John the Baptist and St. Stanislaw were destroyed in August," Ish reminded him.

"Yes, but there were some remains," he protested. "This rubble was made from recent explosions. You can still smell explosive residue from the bombs. There's nearly total destruction of brick gothic structures dating from the 13th century. Look, only one wall of that church has managed to survive." He pointed to the lonely brick wall now supporting nothing.

"This is deliberate, wanton destruction to obliterate centuries of Polish statehood," Frederic said. "But we will rebuild!" he shouted. "When these monsters are no more, the people of Poland will rise, defy these ruins, and bring life from these ashes." His lips tightened, as he glared at the sight before them. Then his face reddened as he became aware of the political sound of his outburst.

"My father told me about a semicircular, fortified outpost he saw when he first arrived in Warsaw," Jack added. "He mentioned rounded turrets capped with cone-shaped, tiled roofs, and arches over the entrances."

"Yes, the Warsaw Barbican. It was a historic fortification located outside Old Town that once encircled Warsaw. It was also destroyed earlier this year," answered Frederic.

"Ish, how do you propose we start to look for your brother?" Jack wanted to change the subject, and, also, he was feeling uneasy standing in plain view. The streets seemed deserted, but snipers could be hidden anywhere. A race of people who rained such horrendous tragedy on inanimate objects would think nothing of getting in a little target practice on innocent stragglers.

"I think we should split up," Ish began. "If I wear my monk's hood and robe and linger around what's left of the foundation of the church, I shouldn't raise any eyebrows. And I'll watch the houses I can observe from there and see if anything arouses my curiosity."

"I'll take two streets over and watch houses there," Frederic volunteered. "What about you, Jack?"

"I'm going to just walk through the ruins two streets in the opposite direction," Jack said.

"Uncover your blonde hair," suggested Ish, "and strut like a German soldier in civilian clothes looking for something to steal."

"Ouch, Ish," responded Jack, "that's a role I'm unwilling to play."

"Sorry, Jack," said Ish, "just some bile humor spilling out."

"Ok. Let's meet back at the truck before dark. If any of us find something suspicious, we can determine our next move." Frederic then turned away from the others to follow the path he had chosen.

Cold, tired, and discouraged the men sat in the cab of the truck eating cheese sandwiches washed down with icy water.

"We have to find shelter," Frederic began as he joined Ish and Jack as the sun dipped low. "We'll be no good to any one if we freeze to death."

"And we can't all wear monk's robes," Jack smiled at Ish.

"If you're ready to convert, you may have my disguise."

"Guess not yet, but it sure looks warm!"

"I've been on business for the old Count several times in this section of town. There's a craftsman here that makes fine jewelry. The Count sent the Zurowski jewels here for cleaning before the war. They were hidden with Stefan when he left Poland for America," said Frederic.

"You think he can be trusted?" asked Ish.

"Yes, he's an honest man. When he'd finished his task, he delivered the jewels to me while being in danger of getting hit when the Germans first started bombing Danzig. I'll go to his house and see if he'll open the door to me," Frederic said. "Maybe he'll know someone who will rent us some space."

"If he's still alive," Ish said, bluntly.

"There is that, of course, but it's all I can think of right now." Frederic pulled his cap closer around his ears, got out of the truck, and walked in the direction where he thought the man lived. Landmarks had been obliterated, but he remembered the general direction, and the front door had been painted dark green with gold letters simply saying, 'Wójcik the Jeweler.'

The green paint was a little faded and the finish of the door was pock-marked by debris that had bounced off it, but the gold letters were still legible. Looking around to see if anyone had shown any curiosity, he saw no one at all. He knocked on the door. There was no answer. After he'd knocked twice more, he turned to leave.

"Mr. Dębręwśki?" A man's hand appeared on the edge of the door as it opened slightly.

"Yes, Frędrić Dębręwśki," he answered softly.

"Quickly, please, come in."

Frederic entered a darkened room with only a small lamp on a table holding the tools of the jeweler's trade. Everything was in neat order, but the house had a slight musty smell from being closed to outside air. The odor was dispersed somewhat by the small fire in the fireplace grate.

"What brings you here? Is the young count with you?" he asked. It was plain to see that the man was uneasy.

"No, he is in residence at the castle," Frederic answered in terms that would assure the old man. "All is well at Domani z Camin. It is being restored."

"That is good," he said.

"Mr. Wójcik, I wish to find a place to stay for a few nights. Do you know of a place nearby that I can rent? I have two friends with me."

The man standing before him was a ghost, a shade from his past. Deep lines on his face mapped the suffering he'd endured, and the eyes had lost their ability to see anything beyond the dismay of his surroundings.

"I'm alone. You are welcome here. My wife and children…." he spoke as he waved his arm toward the pictures on the wall, "are no more."

"Your grief is my grief, Mr. Wójcik," whispered Frederic and he touched the man's shoulder.

"Yes, yes," the man acknowledged, stepping back to allow Frederic to come further into the room. "I have room."

The room was dark, and Frederic noted that much of the furnishings were missing, but there was light coming from another room. A few hydropower plants must still be operating.

A building behind Wójcik's frame house was large enough to conceal their truck. Evidence showed that this had once been a facility for public conveyances. Rubble lay all around, but the doorway was wide enough to allow them entrance. Ish and Jack unloaded what they needed from the truck while Frederic talked with their host.

"Yes, the old Count is gone," said Frederic. "In September '39, young Stefan went home to Domani z Camin and found all of his family members slaughtered along with many of those living on the estate. The Russian soldiers had attacked, showing no mercy."

"We did hear of the attack on Zurowski land. A few residents there fled to Warsaw to check on the survival of loved ones, but they may have perished with them. They did say that many of the tenants escaped and went into hiding."

"True," said Frederic, "many are now back. The new Count is restoring the lands and castle; and once again, there will be a thriving village on Zurowski lands. I helped Stefan to escape to his relatives in America, and now he is back and vows to stay until it is as self-sufficient as before. Eventually he'll have to return to America to head his Uncle's empire. There are signs now that Hitler's power is slipping."

Wójcik nodded his head in agreement. "I pray that is so."

The evening wore on and hunger reminded them that breakfast at dawn had been their last meal. Wójcik offered the use of his stove and Ish fixed supper from the supplies that Manka had packed. Wójcik was hesitant to join them, but Frederic assured him that there was more than enough. Frederic noticed that the man savored every bite of food.

"Frederic, tell me," Wójcik began, "what brings you to Warsaw now?"

"I'm looking for my younger brother," Ish interrupted. He'd waited as long as he could to get to the point of their trip. "His name is David Jacobson."

"Yes," said Frederic. "We were told by someone who knew of him that he might be in the old part of Warsaw. We've been watching activities around the houses, but they all seem shuttered and abandoned."

"Shuttered, yes," Wójcik chuckled, "but not abandoned. Many are safe houses for those Jews who escaped the last bombardment of the Ghetto. The 'quarantine' posters on their doors are enough to keep the soldiers from entering. The fear of coming in contact with disease is real among the Poles and the Germans."

"Do you suppose I could check the houses in the neighborhood to see if anyone knows of my brother," Ish asked.

"No, you're strangers. I will start inquiries. We have a system of communication within Old Town."

Wójcik drew paper and pen from a drawer and wrote a few lines, and he placed it in a basket and covered it with thick slices of bread. He placed it on a table beside the door. "A lad will come and do the rest."

Wójcik told them that most of his jewelry had been taken by soldiers who went from house to house beating the residents and making off with anything they thought was valuable. He pulled a tray from a hiding place within the wall above the fireplace.

"But they missed this, and I've been passing the time creating more from what little inventory I had hidden." He laid the tray of his creations on the table where the lamplight danced from stone to stone.

"Are these for sale?" asked Ish.

"If you see anything that you want," Wójcik answered, shrugging his shoulders.

"I need to take a present to Manka, my wife," Ish said. "Won't she be surprised? This one, I think." It was an amethyst broach in an antique gold mounting.

"Good surprise, I'd say," chimed in Jack. He eyed a green emerald encircled by diamonds set in a white gold band.

Wójcik nodded and wrapped it carefully in a box. His hand trembled when he accepted the money from Ish and returned the tray to its hiding place.

After the men had retired to the rooms Wójcik gave them, it wasn't hard to relax enough to fall asleep.

He couldn't make out the words, but the last thing that Ish heard was the sound of a young boy whispering, Wójcik's soft reply, and then the door closing quietly. Maybe there would be news of David in the morning.

Chapter 25

A cold dawn broke revealing ice-covered rubble disguised by a light blanket of snow, and dangerous footing would lay just below its surface. Walking would have to be slow and deliberate.

"Mr. Debrewski, there has been some news," began Mr. Wójcik. "None of the houses that were contacted had heard of your brother. But the lad reported one suspicious house. It was shuttered tight, and there was no answer to his knock; but through a back window there was a lighted candle and he could see the outline of a man lying on a cot. He thought he heard a soft moan."

"If it's an injured man, he probably won't be alone," Ish said. "I need to get a look inside. If it isn't my brother, they may know something."

"I gave the boy a note to slip under the door; and if we hear from it, I'm sure we will have an answer for you one way or the other. We must wait. Patrols are still trying to round up escaping Jews. They've stopped breaking into our houses at night, but they continue to check our streets in daylight at random times. Strangers seen about would bring too much attention to our houses."

"I have errands that I must complete," said Frederic, "which require that I go to another part of the city. I think my red armband with Hitler's signature will protect me from the soldiers, and the resistance fighters know me from the supplies that I was able to distribute from Józef Zurowski. A new pastor is appointed to Domani z Camin, and if he meets me at the designated place, then he will return with us to the estate. I have also heard that there may be a doctor and his family with them needing to get out of Warsaw."

"I think it will be safe for me to go with you," said Jack. "I'll have my red armband." He didn't want the older man out in the streets alone.

"And you can let your blonde hair shine," Ish offered, "and your blue eyes twinkle." Even the little jeweler joined their laughter.

"Well, it's sure you can't go!" Jack fired back.

It would be a tight squeeze in the truck on the return journey. Jack and Frederic had returned about dusk with the Presbyterian minister, his wife, and young daughter. The doctor was present and relieved at the chance for escape. He was a small, thin man dressed as a priest, and his wife clad as a nun. Both carried black medical bags. The minister was a short man dressed in a long, black robe and gleaming, white clerical collar. His wife and daughter were both covered from head to toe in dark-colored cloaks, protecting them from prying eyes as well as the biting wind.

A hot, goulash stew furnished from Manka's packages sent the spicy odor of paprika, caraway seed, and other fragrant ingredients throughout the house. Ish had built the stew after breakfast, and it had simmered in a large kettle on the back burner of the woodstove. There was still enough of Jack's wood left in the back of the truck to make a good fire.

Frederic introduced the doctor and the pastor as they began to sit at the table. He'd looked around at the place the families had been staying, and the lack of provisions had been plain. He knew they were all hungry.

"As Pastor Angus is to take over from my feeble efforts," said Jack, "it's only right that he starts immediately. Let's ask him to say Grace before we eat. Then perhaps he and our new doctor will introduce their families to the others."

Pastor Angus offered the blessing for the food with open thankfulness. When he raised his head, he turned to his family.

"Thank you all for allowing us to be here. I'm Angus Stewart, and this is my wife, Elsie, and daughter, Skye. She's six years old," the pastor turned to each as he mentioned her name. Mother and daughter had the same golden blonde hair and deep blue eyes, contrasting with the freckled, red-haired pastor with light blue eyes.

"We're most grateful for the offered sanctuary. I'm Doctor Marcin Kawalski. This is my wife, Barbara. She's also a nurse." He stood, and his hand trembled as it gripped the back of his chair.

Supper was quiet as the comfort from the stew nourished body and soul. When the meal was over, they sat drinking coffee. Ish passed around a plate of Manka's apricot-filled angel cookies.

"Momma, look, a cookie," the little girl held it out to her mother as her eyes widened.

"Yes, dear," she answered her daughter. She turned to Ish, "We thank you for such a lovely meal." She patted her mouth and her eyes with her napkin.

"Yes, indeed," the Kawalskis echoed.

Ish allowed Elsie and Barbara to help with the cleanup. Talk after supper was of Domani z Camin, a description of the progress at the estate, and the people now working there.

"Is the castle enchanted?" Skye asked, timidly ducking behind her mother when Ish looked her way.

"Enchanted?" echoed Ish. "It may be enchanted, but it isn't haunted. Happy people live in this castle who will welcome you. There is a school with a lot of children to play with."

It satisfied her question. She rested her head against her mother, covering her mouth as she yawned.

Skye's yawn reminded them that it was time to call it a night. The trek through the city walking against the blustery wind had taken its toll on the new families. Jack and Frederic, too, were ready to turn in even though it was just dusk. Wójcik's offered accommodations for the refugees was the comfort of only one warmed room. A blessing far above the hardships they'd been enduring.

Ish stayed in the dimly-lit living room with Mr. Wójcik waiting for word about the man who lay on the cot in the shuttered house. He couldn't stay seated but paced back and forth from his chair to the window until complete darkness fell.

The wind masked the sound of the knocking, but they saw a folded piece of paper as it slipped under the door. Mr. Wójcik picked it up and stood near the light.

"Well?" ask Ish.

"It is good news and it is bad news," answered Mr. Wójcik. "It is your brother, but he is injured. His companions are doing all they can, but they have no medicine."

"Can I go to him?"

"Yes. They write that someone will meet you at ten o'clock in the building where your truck is parked."

"Okay. I'll get ready," Ish's shoulders relaxed.

"You'll need to go alone," Wójcik said.

"Yes, I've thought of that. I'm willing to put myself in danger, but not the doctor."

Ish filled a flask with hot broth and one with coffee. He had the medical bag that Stanislas had prepared. He made sure that he had the instructions that the doctor had written. He didn't know what he'd find, but he should be able to help.

He donned his monk's hood and cloak again and laced up his boots he had warming by the woodstove. He shoved everything into a duffle bag and waited for the time he was to leave. The little jeweler had warned him that it might be a trick, but the risk had to be taken.

It was David. He was smaller than Ish remembered and his hair had turned white. In his mind's eye, his little brother had been larger than life, ready to take on the world. He had taken it on, and now it was beating him.

"David, David," Ish knelt beside the cot and spoke to his brother.

David's eyelids fluttered in answer to the sound, but his eyes didn't open. Ish squeezed David's hand and felt a weak response.

"David, I'm here. I'm going to look at that wound and see if we can get you back on your feet," he spoke with a conviction he didn't feel.

Shrapnel had embedded in his leg above his knee, and streaks of red shot upward. Infection was setting in and had to be dealt with. Ish turned to the two men in the room.

"What have you been able to do?" He turned to the one standing behind him named Michael.

"Not much," Michael answered. "John and I've packed snow around the wound and tried to keep his fever down with aspirin tablets."

"Good. Can we have some light?" asked Ish.

John brought a lantern and held it above the leg that Ish had uncovered.

"First, I'm going to make sure he doesn't wake up while I work on cleaning this wound."

The two men watched Ish give David an injection. From his duffle, he pulled out some sterile instruments that Stan had prepared and begun the work of cleaning the gash in David's leg. It wasn't a deep wound, but the infection had been the work of the filth clinging to the pieces now lodged in his leg. Poison may have already entered his bloodstream.

He rubbed the area with an antibacterial ointment and covered it with a wide gauze bandage. He took the prepared syringe and gave the injection as Stan had instructed. Stan said it was penicillin, a new medicine dubbed as a wonder drug since it had saved the lives of so many patients in the hospitals suffering from pneumonia and blood poisoning.

"Okay, David, I've done all I can," Ish said. He sat on the floor and leaned back against the cot.

"We're sure glad you showed up," Michael said. The young man was tired and out of his depth. "After we got him here, we didn't know what else to do. It was too dangerous to leave. There's a price on his head, and we were afraid someone might find out he was here."

"I won't leave him now that I'm here," Ish said. "Why don't you men get some rest. Have you eaten?"

"Yes, we still have some provisions, but he hasn't eaten in a few days," John responded. "We could use some sleep."

"When he wakes up, I'll try to get some broth down him and some water. I brought it with me. I'll be here when you wake up. I plan to take him back with me to Domani z Camin."

"He said he knew Count Zurowski. We thought he was joking," John said. "He loved to tease and keep everyone's spirits up."

"No joke. He did know the old count. He also knows Stefan Zurowski, the new count at Domani z Camin. What are your plans?"

"To return to our families. We're both from Krakow and have people there. We wouldn't leave David; but now that you're here, we will try to make it home."

"If you find you need sanctuary, you'll find it at Domani z Camin. I'll be there to welcome you for what you've done for my brother."

Sometime late in the night John and Michael slipped out into the darkness to find their way to Krakow and some safety.

In the early morning hours, David opened his eyes and saw Ish.

"Ish…?" David's voice was weak and hesitant

"Yep, just me," Ish said. "How're you doin', buddy?"

"I thought I saw you, but I thought it was a dream." David turned his head and looked into the room. "Where are Michael and John?"

"Left for home. They started for Krakow during the night."

"That's good," he whispered, "I hope they make it. They risked their lives to get me here."

"Now we have to get you well enough to travel," Ish said, but he knew that David hadn't heard him. He had fallen back to sleep.

He checked the wound again, applied more antibacterial salve, and rebandaged the leg. That done, he pulled a chair close to the cot, got as comfortable as he could, and went to sleep.

Chapter 26

Ordinary snowstorms and blustery winds defined the present winter weather on the estate. Life in the castle village continued as it had over the past generations. Stored forage was put out for the cattle when the snow covered the pasturelands. Stockmen kept track of the newborns in the herds, keeping a running tally of gains and losses. Fences had to be checked and repairs made regardless of weather conditions.

The tannery workers had scraped the beef hides and had made use of the summer sunshine to help remove the unpleasant smell of fresh skins. Now final deodorizing was being done with baking soda solutions before being ready for making into leather items that would be available for sale. A few special preparations had been passed down that allowed some products to fetch a higher price than others. Families who knew these steps guarded their secrets closely.

Stefan had spent the morning in his office meeting with the various managers of the village operations. Progress was being made, but the inability to purchase needed items within Poland slowed things down. Monthly supplies flown in kept things going, but the time lapse between arrivals caused some projects to be put on hold.

The village businesses within the estate weren't self-sufficient yet, but word was getting out that the purchase of necessities was possible again at Domani z Camin. Stefan could see that the funds required from the Zurowski estate were growing less with each passing month. If the trend continued, the village could stand alone financially by summer. After nearly five years those forced to flee were now able to return to the tradition that had bred them.

The thought that his restoration plans for the estate were nearly complete was bittersweet. Only a few hours south of Domani z Camin, Warsaw was still under enemy rule. The security they felt here was a false one. They stayed here unmolested on the whims of a tyrant driven mad by a thirst for utter dominance. His religion was the occult, and his latest icon of power was the Zurowski Jeweled Crucifix which he thought would lead to dominance over all who opposed him.

Stefan had ordered that each house within the village had means of defense in case of attack. They were armed and bunkers had been constructed on the outer edge of the estate borders. It was true that no one had overtly threatened the estate, but Stefan still didn't know the purpose of the man who haunted the woods outside their boundaries. With Frederic, Ish, and Jack gone to Warsaw, Stefan had guards patrolling in the daytime as well as in the night. The prowler was still there, but he stayed outside the borders of the estate. It was as though an invisible wall allowed him to proceed no further; Hitler's edict to ignore Domani z Camin still stood as a barrier. It was reported that Hitler had a fortified bunker near the German border not too far from Zurowski lands where he spent a great deal of time. It stood to reason that he wouldn't want a fight to erupt so closely to his hideaway.

"Stefan?" Sophia questioned as she entered his office.

Stefan stood, went over to her, and held her close. She was his anchor, kept him from drifting. He kissed her tenderly.

"Stefan?' she asked again.

"What is it, sweetheart? I'll give you anything, half of my kingdom," he was snuggling into the softness of her neck.

"I have you. That's enough," she smiled, pulling back gently.

"What is it that you came to ask me?"

"With Jack gone, Monica and Konrad will need an escort to the school. It's a special day for Konrad."

"Yes, I know, it's his fourth birthday," Stefan said, still puzzled. "You have a special time planned for tonight."

"But to Konrad, going to school today is more important. His birthday is being celebrated by his little classmates. Kasia and Manka have made treats and fancy paper hats for the children. The story lady has a special story with new costumes for her and Konrad."

"Story lady?" asked Stefan.

"Monica helps out at the village's day school as the story lady. She and Jack have been taking Konrad to this school twice a week, and once a week she tells a different fairytale. The stories come from the Polish Fairytale book she found in the library."

Stefan sat down, stunned. *Why hadn't he known? Had he been so caught up in the business of the estate that he wasn't aware of what his children were doing? After Konrad began to talk again, he'd just assumed that things had taken care of themselves. He wasn't aware that others were taking over his family obligations. Not really obligations, but opportunities. Opportunities to make memories—for himself as well as Konrad and Jan. Was he becoming his father?*

"When do we leave?" Stefan bounded to his feet.

"You'd better dress warmly," Sophia warned. "The carriage is the mode of transportation today. The princess has to arrive in style." Sophia laughed at the suspicious look Stefan threw her way. "The treats are all packed and in the carriage."

"A princess, huh? Well, tell her highness to wait until I get ready," Stefan was laughing as he rushed from the room.

His trousers were tucked into his boots, and he wore a warm, high-crowned calpac on his head. He put on a long, lined undergarment, then a robe with its sleeves cut from the armhole to the elbow, and a wide ornate sash encircled his waist. He held a fur-lined cloak over his arm. He looked in the mirror and saw his grandfather.

He rushed down and faced Sophia.

"You look gorgeous, even if you smell a little like mothballs," she laughed. "They're waiting in the carriage."

The carriage sported a large flag with the Zurowski Crest followed by small flags with pictures of birthday cakes painted on them. Stefan chuckled under his breath at the thought that his own father would probably have shot the carriage driver.

Proudly, Konrad held his father's hand as he introduced him to his friends. The little ones stood in awe of the new count in his old-world finery. Their shyness wore off as Stefan participated in their games. It would be a day they would never forget, nor would Stefan.

After the small cupcakes were admired and eaten, Stefan saw that the children's eyes never left Monica's face as she skillfully unfolded the fairytale. Konrad slept on the way home, his head resting against Stefan's shoulder.

"Thank you," Stefan said as he looked toward Monica on the other side of the carriage. "Thank you."

A feeling of camaraderie warmed the ride home.

Supper was served early to allow Konrad, Jan, and Sarah to celebrate Konrad's birthday. Ish, Frederic, and Jack were still not back from Warsaw, and Stefan was starting to get concerned. He also noticed that Monica was growing especially quiet during their gatherings in the evenings. Sophia had told him that she thought Monica missed Jack. Jack would be leaving soon, and he hoped Monica wouldn't be hurt. She'd made the trip here with a courage that surprised him.

"Let's put the boys to bed," Stefan said. Konrad laughed as Stefan hoisted him up onto his shoulders. Sophia picked up Jan and followed them out of the room, Sarah trailing behind. Their laughter echoed back to those at the table.

"I'm calling it a day, too," Manka said. "Too much birthday!"

"I agree," Kasia added.

The two women went separate ways to their bedrooms, leaving Stan and Leah lingering over coffee and their pieces of cake.

"Do you think Ish will find my father?" asked Leah. "It's been so long."

"They've only been gone a few days," said Stan.

"No, I mean so long since I've seen him." Leah's voice caught on the words. "If he's gone, then I have no one."

"Leah, that's not true," hurt tinged his words. "You have me. I'm your husband," Stan's eyes sought hers. "In a few short days, our baby will make his or her way into the world. Your world, my world."

"Why are you so patient with me?"

"Leah, don't you know that I love you? You're good. You're kind to everyone."

"I'm tainted!" The cry ripped from her heart. "I want to love you, but I can't forgive myself."

"Forgive yourself for what? For living? For doing whatever it took to stay alive?" She was silent as he talked, tears running down her face.

"I don't know," she admitted, wiping at her cheeks.

"I'm tired of sleeping on that uncomfortable cot. Tonight, I'm sharing your bed," Stan said.

"The baby...," she hesitated.

"I only plan to hold you," he offered his hand. "I want to wrap my arms around my family."

She took his hand and allowed him to lead her to their rooms.

Chapter 27

It had started to snow again, and the truck's snowplow trudged slowly making its own path. The wind billowed the truck's canvas-covered tarp, stretching it tight over the back. The windshield wipers struggled, and every few miles it became necessary to stop and wipe the blades and scrape the snow off the front window. The heater in the truck barely kept the men from freezing.

David Jacobson had been put in a sleeping bag and smuggled out of Warsaw in a body bag. Ish Jacobson, in his monk's hood and robe, stood beside the men as they placed the 'body' in the back of the truck. A pallet of blankets had been placed in the middle of the floor for the injured man. Seated on benches on either side, wrapped in woolen blankets were the Stewarts and the Kawalskis, five bodies trying to combine their heat, huddled as near as possible to the truck's cab. Ish was lying on the floor beside David, holding him to absorb the shocks from the icy-edged ruts in the road.

Jack and Frederic rode in the cab. Frederic pointed the way and Jack wrestled to keep the truck under control. Gusts of wind threatened to make it airborne, and gutted potholes bounced them on frozen tires.

"Will we make the cabin by dark?" Jack asked Frederic. He knew it would be another day before they reached the estate, and Frederic had planned for them to shelter in the cabin again. No stops were planned for food or rest, so it became increasingly necessary that they reach the midpoint back to the estate soon.

"Just before dark, I should say," Frederic answered.

The cabin was a welcome dark cutout against a gray sky. No tracks were anywhere near it, no sign of life showing at the windows. Jack backed the truck up as close to the back entrance of the building as he could and helped them get the injured man inside.

The others grabbed their few belongings and pushed against the wind into the cabin. Jack went to the woodshed behind the cabin to retrieve the axe he'd left there on their trip to Warsaw. Antoni had been able to chop more wood before taking his family on to Domani z Camin, and there was enough for Jack to get a fire started. It wouldn't be enough for the night, but he'd be able to get more cut before total darkness. Some pieces were too wet and would need to dry by the fire.

"I couldn't have done any better with the patient," Dr. Kawalski said as he rewrapped the bandage around David's leg. "He's dehydrated, and we need to get some fluid in him."

"When we get to the estate, Dr. Janda can put in an IV," Ish said.

"Oh, the clinic is equipped?" Dr. Kawalski asked, an expression of interest on his thin features.

"State of the art, doctor," Ish assured him, "state of the art."

David had roused and looked around while his wound was tended. His face was flushed and his eyes unnaturally bright.

"Ish?" he asked.

"I'm right here, little brother," Ish said, kneeling beside the cot. "Right here."

David looked at those around him, "Is everyone safe?"

"All safe. We'll be at Domani z Camin by evening tomorrow. We'll tuck you away in the priest's hidey-hole" Ish tried to talk around the lump in his throat.

He had pulled out all the remaining provisions, and the stew he made was enough for each one to have a cup with the last of

Manka's rye bread. Morning breakfast would be only coffee and the remaining cookies. It would be more food than these people had seen during most days.

He supported David as he was able to take a few sips of broth before losing consciousness again. He arranged the blankets over his brother.

The warmth from the fireplace and the body heat from nine people made this small one-room cabin comfortable for sleeping.

A fire just large enough to make coffee was rekindled in the fireplace. They stowed their few belongings again in the back of the truck. Jack added a shovel of snow to the glowing embers and looked around. The cabin was empty now except for a small stack of firewood left for the next visitors seeking shelter. The trip was taking its toll on Frederic and Ish, and they didn't protest as Jack again climbed into the driver's seat.

David Jacobson had roused when they changed the dressing on his leg, but he was no longer unconscious, sleeping normally. Ish took his place again holding his brother, absorbing the shocks for him.

The howling of the wolves at dusk made for restless sleep within the cabin. When the howling resumed at dawn everyone was anxious to leave the area as soon as possible. Mating season for wolves was still nearly a month away when they became most active, but if a pack were hungry, they would hunt. Some wolves were known for surplus killing, leaving more than they could eat.

The wind had laid down and was no longer drifting snow. The entire landscape up to the edge of the woods was iced over, and fog floated like ectoplasm between the naked limbs. The truck tires crunched the crust of the road as they edged their way home toward the estate. Ish had put the last can of fuel in the tank, and he hoped it would be enough.

Frederic was first to catch sight of the beginning of the Zurowski land. It wouldn't be long before the gothic castle would appear through the rising mist. It might appear ghostly to the new arrivals, but to Frederic it was a safe haven.

"There's where the road branches off to enter the estate land," Frederic pointed to an upcoming fork in the road. This was the first choice they'd had to leave the road they had traveled away from the cabin.

"Good," Jack sighed his answer, as he looked where the other man pointed. "Wait, Frederic, what is that object there by the signpost?"

They drove closer, then a gunshot rang out, and the thing they'd been looking at slumped in a heap in the snow.

"Got him," Ish yelled at them from the back of the truck.

He could see it clearly and had made a clean shot as Jack had turned the truck heading onto the Zurowski road.

Jack stopped the truck, and he and Frederic got out.

"It's a wolf. A large one." Ish had joined them. "Such a nice, thick fur. We'll take it to the tannery." He started to roll the animal over and saw blood on its muzzle.

"Wait, there's something under it."

"It's a man!" Jack gasped.

"It's one of our guards," Ish sighed heavily. "But the wolf didn't kill him. Someone has left a knife in his back. The wolf probably scared him away. It's clear a horse has been here, and the killer has probably been scouting out the estate border."

The men wrapped the dead man in a blanket and fastened the body to the side of the truck. Frederic knew that this guard had lost his family in the Warsaw Ghetto, and there was no one left to mourn him. He could take his final rest at Domani z Camin.

Chapter 28

The relief at their homecoming was shattered by the murder of the guard. The doctor signed a death certificate, and they took the body to the village undertaker.

In the clinic Leah faced Stan, "Death is a lean, tall woman who wears a white sheet and holds a scythe. No human can stop her, but animals can see her and can warn others of her presence. It was better that the guard's death was quick."

"Isn't that a bit morbid?" questioned Stan.

"Perhaps," she paused, "but this is a belief held by Poles in the rural areas as well as in some cities. Maybe the wolf sensed the man's death was imminent and was drawn to him after he was killed."

"Leah, I think it's time for your afternoon rest," Stan urged. She'd been needing more rest as her delivery time drew nearer.

"Don't worry, Stan. I'm okay. Do you know what his funeral will be like?" asked Leah. "The other guards knew him and said he was Catholic. So, I guess the priest that came with Ish from Warsaw will preside."

"The old ways are a common practice in the village," Ish explained. "They will hold a wake in the house where the guard was living here on the estate. Since his family are all dead, his fellow guards, neighbors, and friends will gather for three days to pray for his departed soul. There may even be wailing and singing to keep the bad spirits away."

"There is a procession," Ish continued, "as the coffin is carried on foot to the church where his friends will have a remembrance service. They then walk to the cemetery burial site, the coffin is lowered into the ground, and there is another funeral reading."

"Each mourner will throw a handful of dirt on the coffin before final burial, and a cross with a nameplate is placed on top of the grave with flowers and wreaths," Leah finished.

"Quite a lengthy ceremony," said Stan. "But there may not be too many who knew him well enough to speak for him."

"Will we be expected to attend?" Stan asked.

"No, the Count and Countess will be expected at the remembrance service but no one else is required to go."

Leah sighed, and Stan watched her walk from the clinic. She was still his Viking princess, standing straight and tall, graceful even as she balanced her extra weight.

"Stefan is becoming more watchful of his boys, especially Konrad," Jack said. "With the guard killed, he thinks there's a good chance that the intruder is hiding somewhere close. And he may be right. There are many places even around the castle he could hide and never be noticed."

Jack had tried to find Stanislas alone ever since he'd returned from Warsaw. Stan and Leah spent the mornings in the clinic introducing arriving patients to the new Dr. Kowalski and Nurse Barbara, so there'd been little free time. Now they were alone.

"I know. But he still thinks the intruder on the grounds threatens Konrad," Stan agreed. "Leah is convinced he's after her. She doesn't need this stress so close to the time for the baby to be born."

"Well, whomever he may be threatening, we must be on guard. I'm not leaving for Scotland until after Christmas, so you can count on me to keep an eye out for him. I guess we're still looking for the young man with the scar on his face," Jack said.

"Leah was sure of the description the first time we saw him. Nothing has changed," said Stan. "I've promised to keep her kidnapping a secret, and I'll not betray her."

"Neither will I," Jack looked straight into Stan's eyes.

"But we have no proof that the stalker isn't watching Konrad. I'm sure more than one Nazi soldier has a scar on his cheek. We can only be alert to those around Leah as well as Konrad." The men shook hands on this agreement, and Jack left the clinic feeling that the burden on his shoulders was now shared.

Chapter 29

"Chrithmas is comin'! Chrithmas is comin'!" Konrad hadn't let his lisp curb his exuberance. Jan grabbed Konrad's shirt as they danced up and down. "I'm goin' to be the Mouse King!"

"Me mouse," Jan said. Once he'd found his tongue, the two-year-old had joined in all the conversations.

"Aunt Monkey, who you goin' be?" Konrad was seriously waiting for Monica's answer.

"I'll be Marie," announced Monica.

'Yah!" yelled Konrad, Jan added his echoed, "yah."

"You haf to marry the Nutcracker prince, Aunt Monkey," Konrad giggled as he continued bouncing about.

Although December 6 was the official celebration of St. Nicholas, Monica wanted to stretch the enjoyment of the holidays for these little ones. She was to tell a story on the day before Christmas Eve when village's school was dismissed for the holidays. When the teacher told her that the original story of The Nutcracker was written by a clerk named Hoffman, working in Warsaw, she knew that no other story would do.

Monica had offered fairytales during the year to give the children a way to escape from the bad news they heard at home about the conditions in Warsaw. Something to soften the blow when a relative didn't come home.

Each little girl would wear a crown that she'd made in class, and the boys would wear hand-made mouse ears fastened on a band that went around their heads. Sophia made a tall, fur-covered hat for Konrad and a sheath for his wooden sword. She made a gray, furry costume to turn Jan into a mouse.

Monica had presents for the children. She'd commissioned the estate woodshop to make individual nutcrackers for the children which she wrapped together with her grandmother's gifts of hats and mittens. Jack had cut down a tree, and it stood in the corner with each little gift beneath it. Embroidered and crocheted decorations made by Kasia and Manka were bright against the spreading green branches.

Monica, costumed as Marie, sat in a low chair with the children on the floor in a semi-circle around her. Jack had come to the party dressed as The Nutcracker Prince and sat in the back with Sophia dressed as a dancer. Manka and Kasia made cookies cut out like little nutcrackers and iced with vivid colors, so they came dressed as bakers with sparkling white aprons and chef hats.

As a nod to Christmas in America, the Zurowski carriage was decorated as a bright red sleigh. The team didn't seem to mind that the bells on their harnesses jingled every time they moved, and the old carriage driver smiled at such strange activities.

Manka and Kasia got in on one side of the carriage, and Sophia settled a sleepy Jan and a tired Konrad on the other carriage seat beside her. The driver pointed the horses toward the castle. He would come back for Jack and Monica. It would be dusk soon. The moon was bright tonight, but Stefan had ordered that the boys never be out after dark.

Clean-up was over, and Monica and Jack watched as the last of the children left for home. Some walked and some were picked up in wagons. The teachers lived in small houses nearby.

They heard the jingling of the bells on the horses' harnesses before they saw the lanterns mounted on the sides of the carriage as it rumbled toward them.

"Milady, your carriage awaits," Jack bowed, opening the door for Monica. Her hand was warm in his as he helped her in and settled a carriage robe over them both. He leaned close to her ear. "Konrad whispered a secret to me."

"He did?" asked Monica. When she turned her head, he was close and her eyes went to his lips. *How would it be if she just touched her lips to his?*

"He said Marie has to marry the Nutcracker prince," Jack began. "Did you know that?"

Monica couldn't speak. In the closeness of the carriage, she wanted to throw herself into his arms, and shout *'yes I know that'!* But for the first time in her life, she was shy.

"Well, you're Marie and I'm The Nutcracker Prince, so what should we do?"

"What do you want to do?" Monica's eyes searched his, her voice just a whisper.

"I want to marry you, sweep you up in my arms, and carry you off to the Highlands with me," Jack's hands covered both of hers. "Are you willing, lass?"

"Oh, Jack, so willing."

When he took her in his arms and kissed her, she felt things she'd only dreamed could come true for her. He held her and made her feel like she belonged to him, and that he was hers.

Jack pulled back and reached into his pocket. The ring glistened in the moonlight from the carriage window.

"Jack, how beautiful. Where did you get it?"

"Well, there's this little jeweler in Warsaw…" Their laughter echoed in the carriage as he slipped the ring on her left finger. A perfect fit.

Chapter 30

Bruno had sent him and told him not to come back without her. He'd been suspicious that the girl he brought back from Jedwabne was now carrying his child, and he wasn't going to let her escape. But she had gotten away when the camp was attacked, and Fritz knew he couldn't go back without her if he wanted to live. Bruno was an ugly man with a disposition to match. His men obeyed him out of fear. To go soft over this girl was completely out of character.

He knew Hitler's High Command had declared Domani z Camin off-limits and that some had found sanctuary there, so that was where Bruno sent him. The Resistance Fighters were a threat Fritz had to be aware of in the woods surrounding the road to the estate. He was still a German and knew only a little of the Polish language.

When he arrived at Domani z Camin, he'd posed as a refugee looking for a blonde, girl who'd run away. Dummpkof! As he thought back, he should have just said he was looking for his sister, but it was too late now.

Before the guards were posted, he could have continued to peer into the windows of the cottages. As it was, he had been spotted. His questions had aroused too much suspicion. He was about to venture closer to the castle when he had to retreat outside the boundaries of the estate.

Luck hadn't totally deserted him, though. He found a guard asleep at dawn and knifed him before he could defend himself. But now he was on foot. The wolf he'd seen earlier came bounding out of the forest and spooked his horse, and he'd watched helplessly as his mount disappeared into the trees. As the wolf began to gnaw at the dead man's body, Fritz escaped into the woods. All wasn't lost; at least now he was back on estate property. But when the horse ran away, it had taken the last of his food with it. He'd have to play his refugee role again. He might not be recognized; he now had a beard and his hair was much longer than before. Hair wouldn't grow over the scar, so there was still a chance someone could recognize him.

He'd heard the truck enter the estate road and knew he could follow its trail through the ice-covered road, leaving no tracks in the packed snow. It was too bad losing his mount, but a stranger riding a horse through the village would be suspicious. If he did find the girl, he would need to steal a vehicle to take her back to Bruno at the army camp.

He heard it stop, and he decided that someone had rescued the guard's body from the predator. He could see several people inside were huddled under blankets as though they'd traveled a distance. Good. Huddled together for warmth, they wouldn't be looking out his way.

No one had seen a blonde runaway, or if they had, they weren't talking. Bruno had reminded him that she was a nurse, so she might seek employment at a medical facility. Help in these places was needed badly with no references necessary. He'd seen villagers going into the clinic at the castle. It had a door facing into the courtyard and one small window. He'd seen a brown-haired man with a stethoscope around his neck, so they had at least one doctor. He'd not seen the nurse.

One person told him that the doctor's wife was blonde. He didn't set much hope on this information, but he'd get a look at her before giving it all up. He wouldn't be going back under Bruno's command if he didn't have the girl. He knew he'd be hunted but running would be his only chance of survival.

A light shone out of the small window of the clinic. Carefully, Fritz edged his way along the hedgerow up to the last bush just under the window. He looked in. A woman, dressed as a nurse, was standing with her back to the window talking with another woman. Soon the other woman left the room, leaving only the doctor and nurse alone.

The doctor walked over to the nurse and gently turned her to face him and kissed her.

It was Leah. He'd found her. And she was with child. This had to be Bruno's baby. He saw a ring on her hand and the man was rubbing his hand over her large abdomen. When this man married Leah, he'd signed his death warrant. Now he'd just have to plan how best to kill this man and take Leah away before raising any alarm. She'd been here for many months and, obviously, had people who cared for her.

Fritz could be patient. It was about over. He wanted to go home to his family in Germany; he didn't want to be forever on the run in Poland looking over his shoulder. From his hiding place in the courtyard, he watched the lights go out in the clinic and the shade pulled down over the window, and he heard the lock click as the door was secured. Since they didn't come out, he knew that they had their rooms inside the castle itself. No matter. He'd found a way that led into the dungeon area of the castle. It wasn't the way he preferred to enter, but it was deep under the upper area and sound would be absorbed in the damp, earthen tunnel.

He crawled as close as he could to the entrance into the castle proper without actually entering. The Knight's Hall must be directly above him because he could hear the muffled sounds of voices, laughter, and knew that they were sitting down to supper. The pangs in his gut burned with hatred for the diners. How long had it been since he'd eaten?

He listened closely and could pick out Leah's voice. She'd bid everyone goodnight but urged her husband to stay and have dessert. This would be perfect. He listened as her footsteps disappeared and the voices continued.

The shadows in the far end of the Knight's Hall were enough to conceal him, and he made his way through the nearest exit which he guessed led to the upper bed chambers. Luck was still with him. He saw a light glimmer under a door and someone was humming on the other side.

The knob turned smoothly and the door opened silently.

"Ready to go back, Leah?" Fritz snarled.

"Fritz," gasped Leah, she hugged her arms around her.

"No other," he sneered. "Bruno wants you back. And that brat you're carrying."

She opened her mouth to respond, but he held up his hand. "No more. Time to go. Get a coat on."

Suddenly, she bent nearly double and the scream that ripped from her throat echoed down the corridor to the Knight's Hall. Water gushed down her legs and puddled around her feet. She reached for the bedpost to steady herself.

He ignored her unbalance, grabbed a blanket from the bed, and put it around her. "Hurry. Outside. Now." He pushed her in front of him, holding a gun to her head. Gripping her tightly, he wrapped his arm around her smashing her swollen breasts.

"Fritz, I can't..." she fainted and sagged to the floor, leaving her assailant an easy target. He panicked and his shot entered the wall high above those now facing him.

Another shot rang out and Stefan held the smoking revolver in his hand, Jack and Stan were on either side of him, holding guns that didn't need to be fired.

"We don't have to worry about our stalker anymore." Stefan leaned against the door frame. "He just looked in the wrong room."

They watched Stefan go to the room where his boys and Sarah slept to check on them. Neither Jack nor Stan would tell him that the stalker had found the exact room he was looking for.

Leah roused and Stan picked her up and started for the clinic. "Here we go, sweetheart, time to welcome our baby."

"Don't worry, Leah," Stefan said, "we'll prepare a new suite of rooms for you to come back to."

After Stefan checked on the sleeping children, he quickly summoned the guards. Tomorrow would be soon enough for an investigation to determine how the stalker gained entrance, but tonight he just ordered the cleanup and a quick burial of the man outside the borders of the estate.

He and Jack returned to those waiting downstairs. They'd all moved from the Knight's Hall to the side room where they gathered every night after supper.

Frederic and Ish still had their guns drawn.

"All's well now. The stalker won't give us any more concern."

"Thank God, our boys are now safe," Sophia's whisper was a prayer of thanksgiving. "Do you know who he was? Do you know who sent him?"

"He didn't give us an opportunity to question him, but we did see a swastika tattoo on his wrist. He'll not be buried on Zurowski land." When this young man didn't return to his family after the war, perhaps they'd mourn, but Stefan knew that no one at Domani z Camin would feel sorrow for him.

"And Leah?" asked Manka.

"She wasn't injured, but Stan has taken her to the clinic. She's gone into labor." He turned to Sophia and said, "You might want to have the maids prepare another suite of rooms for Stan and Leah. I don't think they'll feel comfortable going back to their old ones."

"I'll have it attended to right away," said Sophia, glad to have something to do.

"Oh, baby clothes. We'd better get something ready to take to the clinic," Kasia clapped her hands. "And a gown for Leah." The women had been busy for months sewing a layette.

Any shade of regret here would be overcome by the brightness brought by the new innocent life being birthed into their lives. In this war-torn country, resilience was the word of the day. Each day. And as for law, here at Domani z Camin, Count Stefan Zurowski's word was the law and would go unchallenged.

Sophia ordered coffee and the dessert that they'd missed at supper, and they all sat together before the fire, waiting.

It was nearly midnight when Stan invited them all to the clinic to see his new daughter, whose hair was golden fuzz and whose tiny features were those of the Viking princess lying beside her.

Chapter 31

A hush had settled down on the castle and the surrounding lands. Smoke rose from every chimney, and each household was filled with the aroma of traditional dishes being prepared for the upcoming celebration. Tomorrow would be Christmas Eve. Children played merrily in the snow, and Stefan was feeling a sense of satisfaction. He'd directed the return of all the items his father had hidden in the keep before the onslaught of the Russian army. He'd remembered from his childhood where each piece should go.

Stan and Leah had named their little daughter Noelle, and the christening had taken place in the castle chapel with Pastor Angus guiding the ceremony. David Jacobson, as a proud grandfather, stood at Leah's side, beaming at the baby. The thought that his half-Jewish granddaughter would be reared in a protestant home was of no consequence to him. Leah was alive, safe, with a good husband who was taking her to a new land to be received by his waiting family. He, on the other hand, was dedicated to help in the rebuilding of his homeland, and there wouldn't be room in his life for anything else. He was healing fast, and after Christmas he would return to Warsaw. It was enough to know that his daughter and granddaughter wouldn't be exposed to the life he would be living. Leah's grandparents had been wealthy, but it hadn't protected them from the death camp. And there was nothing to pass on to their granddaughter.

Jack and Monica sat and watched the table being set for the *Wilia* Supper.

"Are you going to help?" asked Jack.

"No. Our grandmother was always in charge of preparing the table, and now Sophia is in charge and will ask if she wants help," she used a voice so low that only Jack could hear. "Although she isn't the oldest, she is the Countess. I want her to have the honor."

"Monica, you work hard at masking your soft heart," said Jack as he placed a kiss on her cheek.

"But I wasn't always successful," Monica sighed, "you found me out."

"I did," he agreed. "And I think Konrad sees his Aunt Monkey for the softie that she is." He ducked as she swung a make-believe blow at his head. He put his arm around her waist and held her close as they watched Sophia continue preparing the table.

Sophia put a thin layer of hay on the top of the long Knight's table and laid a white tablecloth carefully on top.

"What's she doing now?" asked Jack.

"The *Wilia* Supper is a feast commemorating the birth of the God Child, and the thin layer of hay is to help us remember that the Holy Child was born in a manger."

"What a wonderful custom," said Jack. "In Scotland, December 25 isn't even a holiday. The kirk, church to you lass, frowns on such festive occasions. It happened in 1640 during the Protestant reformation. A law was passed making 'Yule' vacations illegal. There were harsh punishments."

"What? Am I marrying a heathen?" Her green eyes widened.

"The ban on Christmas was lifted in 1712, but still festive celebrations were frowned upon. There was a time when there were no gifts given, no Christmas trees, and no Santa Claus coming down the chimney."

"Will I be spending my life with a staid Scotsman?" She rolled her eyes in horror. "How sad."

"Ah, lass, come New Year's Eve, our Hogmanay, there's late-night partying, feasts, gift giving, fireworks," Jack said and added as he leaned closer, "just about anything goes."

"Sounds more like it," she kissed his cheek.

"Ah dinnae ken, lass. You may need to rest up," he laughed as she ducked her head. "Are you blushing?"

"Absolutely not," she denied, "listen as I tell you what they're doing now."

"Those small sheaves of grain, that we tied up yesterday with colored ribbons, are placed in the corners of the room."

Manka was helping Sophia, and as she put each sheaf into its corner, she knelt briefly, crossed herself.

"She's saying a prayer for a good harvest in the next season," Monica explained.

Sophia went to the linen closet and brought out a stack of snowy white napkins with a silver "Z" embroidered in the corner. The silver napkin rings were initialed, also. Sophia and Manka reverently handled the silver and china that they would use at the *Wilia* Supper. They brought the crystal goblets from the glass front cabinet, each one etched with the letter 'Z'.

"These things for the *Wilia* Supper have been stored in the keep. It's hard to predict how old they are, but I watched the laundresses restore the linens, and the butler polished the silver until I thought it would catch fire," Monica continued to talk in a low voice. "These are the originals; Uncle Jósef had duplicates made for the *Wilia* Supper at home in Dark Forest."

A small, delicately carved manger scene was placed in the centerpiece. Mary and Joseph looked over the Baby Jesus, and the shepherds stood at one side with two little lambs. The Three Wisemen knelt at the other side offering gifts; one Wiseman laid down his crown. A star stood directly over where the Child lay by means of a small stiff wire connected to the roof of the stable.

"Uncle Józef told us that he had made this Nativity Scene himself many years ago; he made one for Forest House, too."

"The table looks beautiful," Kasia exclaimed as she came into the room. She walked around the room fingering things as though to draw a blessing from the symbols.

"Thank you," Sophia smiled at the compliment, "I'm going to lie down with the boys for their nap this afternoon."

Manka turned to Sophia, "thank you so much for allowing me to help with the table."

"*And she brought forth her firstborn son, and wrapped him in swaddling clothes, and laid him in a manger; because there was no room for them in the inn,*" Jack's deep voice added the opening lines to the Christmas Story. His face glowed with the power of those words.

"Have I redeemed myself?" he asked softly.

Monica touched her wet cheek and took Jack's hand.

"Remember, the Evening Star is the dinner bell on Christmas Eve!" Sophia gayly called out.

" Konrad, Jan, and Sarah have been looking for the Evening Star ever since lunch. They're so excited." Manka hummed to herself as she turned to put away the extra silver.

Stefan and Sophia had been gathered with the children at the window when the first glow of the Evening Star appeared.

"The star, the star," Konrad shouted, and he and Jan clapped their hands. "Time to eat!"

Everyone gathered in the Knights' Hall waiting to break and exchange the *Ópątek*. These thin, unleavened wafers were stamped with the figures of the Christ Child, the Virgin Mary, or the Holy Angels.

Reverently, Stefan picked up a wafer. He led them in exchanging good wishes as they partook of the wafers. Sophia rested her hand on her husband's arm. She knew that he'd been neglected at Christmas by his father and often excluded from partaking of the Bread of Love.

The table had been set for the family, but an extra place was laid in expectation of the coming God Child. A candle burned brightly in the window to guide any stranger that might be passing into their midst. The stranger might be the God Child in the form of a human man. As was Polish custom, Jósef read a poem to them from a small leather volume.

"When I was a little girl," Mrs. Kowalski's shyness was overcome by her emotion, "we worked the words 'Guest in the home is God in the home' on a small tapestry sampler. The custom of leaving the extra place comes from this ancient Polish adage."

"Yes, there's one hanging here in the castle," Sophia remembered.

"Yes," agreed Stefan. "Uncle Jósef said my grandmother made it when she was a girl."

"We have a similar poem," Jack said,
'Christmas in heaven what do they do?
They come down to earth, to spend it with you.
So, save them a seat, just one empty chair.
You may not see them, but they will be there'."

Although not Catholic, Stefan remembered the first time that Ish had eaten the *Wilia Supper* with them:

"And never should there be an odd number seated at the *Wilia Supper*," Manka protested earnestly. "If there is, someone will not live to see the next Christmas."

"Manka, that's just a superstition," Uncle Jósef had tried to console the woman.

"Remember Sophia's twin brother, Jan! There was an odd number at the table the Christmas before he died. We must not take a chance!" There was fright in her eyes. "Either Ish must be at the table or I must not!"

"But he's not Catholic, he is Jewish. Never before has he participated in the *Wilia* Supper!" Jósef had explained.

"But Ish is Polish!" Manka was adamant.

Jósef agreed to invite Ish and was surprised that the little man accepted. From the twinkle he saw in Ish's eye, Jósef was sure that Manka had done some softening up on her own. So, with the family, including Manka, Antek, Ish, and the Jandas, twelve sat down to supper that year.

As in past years, Manka oversaw the food preparation for the *Wilia* Supper, but this was the first time in the Old Country, and it would be served by the castle staff.

Fish was the basic ingredient for the eleven-course Christmas Eve dinner. The appetizer was pickled herring served with individual salads followed by clear *brąśźćś* and mushroom *uśżką*. There was pike fillet baked with cream and baked sauerkraut and mushrooms. The pike in aspic was nestled beside white mounds of cauliflower with a crumb and butter topping. The fresh fried salmon came with tender potatoes with tomato sauce.

Darkness had come with the night as the dinner progressed. Prune compote preceded poppy seed cake followed by nut pudding. Pastries, nuts, and candies were brought in with the coffee.

It was time to go to Midnight Mass. Ish was staying at the house with his brother David, who was still on crutches. He would agree to eat the *Wilia* Supper with them, but Manka still couldn't persuade him to attend Mass. He promised to keep the fire roaring in the fireplace.

Moonbeams bounced off the Zurowski Crest on the side of the carriage. The Count and Countess would show up in the tradition of generations before. Zurowski children Konrad and Jan, along with Sarah, sat wrapped in the heavy lap robes beside Manka. Although Stefan and Sophia were no longer practicing Catholics, Stefan would never withhold long-held village traditions that offered such comfort to the people.

He'd attended small protestant churches since he was a young man when Fredric had first unfolded the plan of salvation to him through a personal faith in Jesus Christ. Since then, his faith had been his rock.

Father Nowak, the priest who had come to Domani z Camin from Warsaw with Ish, would be conducting the mass. The stable hands were driving horse-drawn buggies to carry the others who wanted to attend. It was snowing only lightly now, but the white ground cover sang of the holiness of the night. A little lamb in the live nativity scene outside the church bleated softly.

Stefan had approved Pastor Angus's plan to hold a Protestant Watchnight Service on New Year's Eve, Hogmanay, the seventh day of Christmastide. The service would include the singing of hymns and testimonies of congregants, and a sermon from the new Pastor Angus. Stefan was looking forward to worshiping in this manner.

The service would be open to all, and he thought that perhaps some of the villagers would like an opportunity to express thanksgiving to God for his blessings over the past year.

Stefan turned his thoughts to the present service. The village church was inspiring: the traditional Nativity Scene and the candles burning. The Christmas Carols were sung by the congregation with lusty, thankful voices. It was the time of prayer, and Sophia knelt beside Stefan in the dimness of the church.

There was another time that he had knelt in another church on a special occasion. Sophia had told him of the time of her proxy marriage to him. He was no more than a name then. The Zurowski attorney, Vincent Ludlow, had stood in his place, as coldly legal as the forms she had signed.

Now, Sophia was familiar, warm, and vital. Stefan reached for her hand in the darkness, and it was there ready to take his into her own. They were one in spirit; he knew that Sophia's mind was thinking back to that time.

Chapter 32

Winter held the estate in a tight grip until the month of April. When the weak sunlight offered some relief, farmers took to their fields, preparing the ground to receive the wheat berry, kernels, and other grain seeds. Cold-weather vegetable seedlings were taken from the greenhouses and put out for the first planting. Orchards were cleared of fallen branches; rows of strawberries were covered by blankets of straw, waiting to burst forth with sweet, bell-shaped berries. Spring was stretching its arms into action. The villagers' work would continue to escalate until the burgeoning crops cried for harvest.

Newborns of all the animals were coming fast at this time of year. Bawling and baaing could be heard coming from pens and pastures. Watches were set to protect the helpless young from roaming predators. Life on the land carried on as it had for generations.

The shrubs and trees in the castle courtyard were clipped into ornamental shapes, and flower beds awakened to bloom when the mild air of May began to warm the soil. Nature had an order that not even man's interference could halt.

Stefan Zurowski looked at the calendar on his desk. He'd marked October 2, 1944, in black. It was the day General Tadeuz Bor Komorowski surrendered Warsaw after Hitler's order for the complete destruction of that city. A straight line was drawn from August 1, through October 1, marking the Warsaw Uprising as those in the Ghetto raged a bloody battle for an independent Poland. The German forces overpowered the city by merciless force. He'd penciled in 150 thousand: the number of civilians reported as killed during that day.

David Jacobson had gone back to Warsaw after his leg had healed, and he reported back that about 90% of Warsaw was destroyed when the Russians and Germans joined together against the Poles. A reward was still offered for David Jacobson. The Nazis learned that he was keeping a diary with dates and occurrences and those responsible for atrocities. David had hidden the diary at Domani z Camin before returning to Warsaw. Only he and his brother, Ish, knew its whereabouts.

The pall of gloom settled as far as their sanctuary here at Domani z Camin. The villager men wore black armbands, and the women tied black scarves on their heads. Stefan decided that the best course was to keep things productive on the estate so that they could continue to funnel food through hidden routes to those starving in Warsaw and surrounding areas. Grain of all kinds was abundant for the needs here, and the overflow would make its way to outlying villages.

David had told them of a top-secret, high-security site in the Masurian woods that wasn't too many miles from the Zurowski Estate. Stefan didn't know if David was part of a failed assassination attempt that took place there or not, but someone had breached the security at what was known as Wolf's Lair shortly after David had rejoined his band of resistance fighters back in Warsaw. Stefan had feared that there might be retaliation on Domani z Camin after this because of its proximity to Hitler's camouflaged bunker, but no threat came. Hitler may have attributed his safety to possessing the Zurowski Jeweled Crucifix.

Stefan knew it was time to plan on going back to America. Uncle Jósef had shouldered too much of the burden far too long alone. Konrad would start school this fall, and Sophia was talking more of Forest House.

Special Envoy Wilhelm Stendal watched his Fuhręr grow edgier as news of defeats were posted. They were at the Wolf's Lair, but it was nearly the end of April, and now he was talking of going back to Berlin. Stendal watched him clutch the Zurowski Crucifix tightly in his hands as he bowed and kissed it before handing it to him. The Fuhręr had dismissed his occult advisers when they had nothing further to offer, but Stendal noticed that the restlessness was still upon their leader. His Fuhręr had left for Berlin to join the German High Command.

The secret task he was to carry out wouldn't be so far away. It was the last effort to gain victory; all of Germany was depending on him. He'd drive his car, his black SS armband on his sleeve, and proudly waving the swastika fastened on the antenna. No one except him knew his destination or what he had to do. The curse of the Zurowski Crucifix had fallen upon them, and it had to be reversed.

Domani z Camin had been declared off-limits, which was the exchange price, but kidnapping the Count's son had annulled the passage of the prosperity and good fortune to the Crucifix's new owner. They had been warned, but only after the kidnapping.

Stendal left the Wolf's Lair before dawn. He knew that it would be nearly dark when he reached the Zurowski Estate and found a hiding place for his car and a way to get in without being seen. The weather was in his favor, and the excitement building inside him gleamed on his face. *This is it. I'll be remembered for all time—savior of the Third Reich, allowing a thousand-year reign.*

The copse of pine left a circle of ground where the car could be hidden. No sounds greeted him when he got out of the car nor did he see any sign of a guard post. His breathing was erratic and his eyes glazed with anticipation.

Fools, he thought. They were feeling very complacent. The war was still raging, and yet here it was peaceful and undisturbed. Well, it could stay that way if they would co-operate. He hefted his bag to a more comfortable position on his shoulder. The bag held the Zurowski Jeweled Crucifix wrapped again in its original box. *If the Count didn't agree to reverse the curse, then the boy must die.*

Stendal could see Count Zurowski through the window seated at his desk. The boy was playing on the floor with building blocks. Fate had set the stage perfectly.

Stendal had scouted earlier and found a door that was unlocked and would lead to the study. He used it, unsnapping his sidearm from its holster.

"Heil, Hitler!" Stendal saluted.

Stephen quickly got to his feet, standing in front of a frightened Konrad. "Good evening, Stendal. What else could you want?"

"It's the bad man, poppa," whispered Konrad, slipping under the desk.

"Not bad," denied Stendal, "I've come to do good." His upper lip disappeared as he tried to smile, looking like his large teeth were growing down from his mustache.

No wonder that Konrad had been afraid, thought Stefan. "What do you want?" Stefan asked, again.

"I want to return the Crucifix," the glitter in his eye was desperate.

Stefan noted Stendal's shaking hand at his weapon and the maniacal aura radiating from him. If only Konrad weren't in the room.

"How thoughtful of you. It has been in our family for generations," Stefan said, calmly. "But what do you want in return?"

Stendal pulled the box from his bag, opened it, and laid it on Stefan's desk.

"Remove the curse," he demanded. "It is causing reversals in our battles. Our armies are experiencing setbacks. Never before have our armies suffered such defeats." His voice raised as he pounded his fist on the desk.

"There's no curse," Stefan denied, softly.

"Of course, there's a curse," he pointed his gun at the desk where Konrad was hiding his face on the floor.

"You put the curse on us when we took your son," Stendal's voice still echoed in the room.

"No," Stefan countered, "you cursed yourself when you did that."

"So, I can lift the curse. I will kill your son," Stendal's words were final and without hesitation, he aimed the gun at the huddled figure under the desk.

Before Stefan could move, a gunshot reverberated throughout the lofty ceilings of the study, followed by a second shot that buried itself high in the wall above Stefan's head.

A look of surprise widened Stendal's eyes as he slumped to the floor. Blood was staining his uniform, and a trickle ran from the side of his mouth as he lay unmoving.

"Aunt Monkey, he was the bad guy," Konrad threw himself into Monica's arms. The gun she'd used lay on the floor beside Stendal. His gun now lay useless in his open fist.

"Yes," she held him tightly, "I told you I wouldn't let him get you again."

"Monica, how did you know?" asked Stefan, who was now cradling his son close to his chest.

"I saw him come in, and I heard Konrad say he was the 'bad' man. The first words he said to me when he woke up from his coma was 'don't let the bad man get me again'. And I promised him." Her voice trembled as she suddenly sat down in the closest chair. "Uncle Jósef said I was the best marksman in our family, and I've been armed most of the time."

"Oh, Monica, are you alright?" moaned Stefan.

"Hey, had to save the future Count Zurowski," she tried to smile at Konrad.

"Just my little boy," Stefan's voice choked.

"I'm okay, poppa. He was a bad man. Don't cry," Konrad said. He patted his dad's shoulder, keeping his face turned from the dead man sprawled before the desk.

"That fool on the floor didn't even know that his brave leader committed suicide in Berlin yesterday," Stefan said.

The noise from the raised voice of the German and the gunshot had brought everyone into the study. Carrying Konrad, Stefan led the way out and into the room where they all usually gathered after supper. The roaring fire helped comfort, but it would be a while before a full account could be given.

Sophia and Stefan held both Konrad and Jan close. Monica nestled in the arms of Jack, feeling reassurance from his closeness. A disaster had been averted this day, and Jack led them all in a prayer of thanksgiving.

The body of Wilhelm Stendal was removed from the study along with all evidence that he'd been there. He would be buried beside the other enemy soldier who'd tried to kidnap Leah. These were just more casualties of war.

Chapter 33

Stefan had noted on his calendar that shelling began in Berlin on April 20, 1945. He had wondered if it was deliberate that the bombing started on Hitler's 56th birthday. He'd written May 2, 1945, as the official surrender of the city, and that note was circled in red.

The news that Berlin had fallen and that Germany had unconditionally surrendered were welcome news here on the estate. Bells rang, patriotic songs, and firecrackers could be heard throughout the night in celebration.

He turned the page to the present, May 9, 1945, and the fighting had now ended in Europe. In a few days, he and those who had come with him would mark their second anniversary here at Domani z Camin. It was time to go back. Frederic had gone ahead of them to take care of some estate matters which he hoped could be finalized when he got to Warsaw. There were plans to be made now that the Crucifix had been returned to Stefan.

Stefan would be leaving Domani z Camin in good hands. Business management was running smoothly under Frederic's control as it had in his father's day, and Frederic was grooming a hand-picked assistant. Ish Jacobson and Manka wouldn't be returning to America; he would be the manager of all the farms, landscaping, and maintenance at the castle and accompanying buildings.

It was later than usual when they all gathered after supper. Spring still dictated a fire in the fireplace, and everyone was seated in their favorite chairs. The children were in bed and the only sound heard was the popping of the fire as the logs burst.

"Time has come to plan on our trip back to the States," Stefan began, "but we don't want to wait until winter when sailing may get rougher."

"I ordered some Mothersill's Seasick Pills that came in on the plane with the last medical supplies," Stanislas joined everyone's laughter.

"Oh, you poor thing," Leah tried to control her giggle.

"Ok, everyone, I'm all set for an ocean voyage. Seriously, Dr. Kowalski is familiar with all the new equipment now and is nearly running the clinic."

"Yes," added Leah, "and Barbara is such a well-trained nurse that it took her no time to grasp our methods. And all the patients love her."

"Frederic and Ish can well run the estate, Manka and Kasia can handle household staff, Pastor Angus and Father Nowak can care for the spiritual needs, and the rest of us must make our departure plans," Stefan said, looking around. "Anyone else staying here?"

"She's with me," Jack pulled Monica to his side, "and she's agreed to become the bride of a highland laird. Ah dinnae ken. It sounds a lot loftier than it is."

"It's to keep you in line," Monica retorted. "And you promised me that we'd do a lot of traveling!"

Congratulations mingled with laughter from everyone.

"Stefan, we want to get married here if that's ok?" Monica was hesitant.

"Monica, are you actually asking my permission on something?" Stefan threw up his hands in surrender.

"What can I say, Stefan," Jack interrupted "she may become manageable yet." Jack ducked a blow from Monica.

"Konrad says the story lady and the prince must get married in the castle," explained Monica.

"So, we thought we'd get married in the courtyard with an open invitation to all in the village," finished Jack.

"I'll love it;" beamed Manka, "think of all the baking we can do." She clapped her hands.

"When do you want this grand affair to take place?" teased Stefan.

"I want to be a June bride," Monica blushed. "Will that be enough time for everything, Manka?"

"Perfect," Manka and Kasia said together.

"Jack and I will be in Warsaw for about a week," said Stefan, "so we'll be out of the way of things going on here."

"Be sure he gets back in time," Monica threatened Stefan, playfully.

"It may be out of my control," retorted Stefan, "Jack is driving his car."

"You have a car here?" Monica's eyes widened. "And you've made me bounce around in that carriage?"

"It was my parent's car. It was stored in a back building here on the estate after his death, and I've just not wanted to use it yet."

"Oh, Jack, I'm sorry," Monica laid her hand on Jack's arm.

"Don't be too quick to forgive me, sweetheart," Jack's voice held laughter. "You haven't seen the car."

"You mean I wouldn't want to be seen in it?" she asked.

"Not exactly that. My dad became a self-supported missionary after he retired, but he could still afford to indulge his passion for a reliable ride. I'll be chauffeuring Count Stefan Zurowski to Warsaw in my dad's old car," Jack continued his teasing tone.

"How old?" asked Monica.

"1940 model--I'm afraid it's five years old," Jack raised one eyebrow as he continued to look at Monica, "but it is a Rolls Royce. My dad's weakness, I'm afraid."

Monica threw a pillow at Jack.

"On that, I'm off to bed," pouted Monica.

"Yes, it's getting late. I'm ready, too." Stefan and Monica left together.

Soon the soft talk and laughter were but echoes and one by one the lights in the room were extinguished as each welcomed the end of another day.

Chapter 34

The chrome on the Rolls winked at those waving good-by to the passengers heading for Warsaw. The black fenders and top had not dulled with dust, and the yellow door panels seemed to borrow color from the sun.

The two men would be able to travel faster alone, but a stop at the halfway cabin would still be necessary. The days were getting longer, and they drove until there was only enough light to find the cabin. They'd arrive in Warsaw before the sun set the next day, where Fredric would meet them at Mr. Wócjąk's, the jeweler.

The Rolls moved smoothly over the cobblestone streets of the Old Town. They'd traveled slowly through the newly-cleared roads, but so much was left to do.

"Jack, did you hear what General Eisenhower said during his visit to Warsaw?" asked Stefan as they drove through unmarked streets.

"I don't think so."

"He said 'Warsaw is far more tragic than anything I have seen…This represents deliberate destruction and the burning out of an entire city by the Germans'."

"He's right. This destruction doesn't represent one country trying to extend its borders to accommodate a growing population of its own, this represents a tirade by a man gone mad with hatred."

It was silent in the car as the men took in the ruins around them.

"There," Stefan pointed to his right, "there is Wócjąk's house."

"Do you think we can park the car where we had the truck last time?" asked Jack.

"Looks like a drive has been cleared, so I think they're expecting us."

"Did Frederic and Ish drive the truck here when they came back?" asked Jack. "I don't see it."

"No," Stefan smiled. "Do you know what they drove?"

"No," said Jack, looking at Stefan for an answer.

"Ish and David found the car in a pine copse where Wilhelm Stendal had hidden it before he attempted to kill Konrad. David stripped all Nazi identifying symbols from it and said it would be put to better use." Their laughter echoed inside the car.

"Good for him. So, David drove Frederic and Ish to Warsaw," Jack said when he could finally talk.

"Yes, and they'll return with us."

The car fit in the garage, allowing the doors to open without touching. The men headed to Wócjąk's house. A light was coming through the window by the door. They knocked, and it opened quickly.

"Gentlemen, come in, we're expecting you," the little jeweler smiled with his greeting. He shook hands with them. "Delighted to have so much company."

Frederic and Ish stood back further in the room.

"Shall we eat," the jeweler smiled, "and then talk business?" His look held meaning for Stefan.

"Thank you. Jack and I were too anxious to get here to stop and fix something," Stefan took the seat the host pointed out and sat down. When everyone else was seated, the food was blessed and the men ate.

After the table was cleared, Mr. Wócjąk left the room and came back carrying two identical boxes. He laid a dark cloth on the table and opened the boxes.

He took pieces from their cases and laid them side by side.

"What do you think, Count?" he asked.

"I think you are a genius," Stefan was in awe, "a true artisan."

On the table before them lay two jeweled crucifixes.

"It was impossible to obtain jewels the quality of those in the original crucifix, but I did find some exceptional stones."

"Yes, you did," Stefan's breath caught. "Stunning."

"No one who hadn't seen the original Zurowski Jeweled Crucifix would be able to tell it from the copy, and I think even those who hadn't seen it recently wouldn't be too sure which was the original.

"You are right," said Stefan. "But, of course, this is the original." He picked up one of the crosses reverently.

"Yes, you would know," the jeweler nodded. "It probably calls out to you as the possessor. There's magic in it."

"Many men have thought so," agreed Stefan. "This commission that I gave you to create a copy is for the protection of the crucifix.

"This, of course, must remain a secret. Only the five of us know that there is a copy: Frederic, Jack, Ish Jacobson, you, and I. It is for the safety of the Crucifix, as well as our safety, that no one else knows.

"Blood has been spilled because of it, an innocent kidnapped, and men are driven mad to possess it. And that's just in the last few years. This Crucifix has encountered much evil as it journeyed through the Middle Ages until now. I think I have a plan to uncloak some of the mystery shrouded around it. Things hidden in the dark whisper of evil for lack of understanding."

"Stefan, you know that you can count on me to never say a word," Jack looked him in the eye.

Frederic, Ish, and Mr. Wócjąk nodded solemnly.

"Frederic will handle your payment," Stefan nodded toward Frederic.

"Already done," Fredric said.

"Good. Thank you," Stefan felt a burden had lifted. "It's been a long day, and I'd like to turn in." He put the two crosses in their boxes and followed his host.

Mr. Wócjąk showed them their sleeping accommodations. Soon all was quiet. Not a sound of war could be heard this night.

Chapter 35

There is no death, there is only the sowing for the harvest of the future.

Stefan Zurowski couldn't remember where he'd heard it or even read it, but it fit the scene as he drove through Warsaw. Warsaw had been dealt a killing blow, but her death wasn't in the cards.

Frederic told him that even before the war, city planners had made new studies to reconstruct Warsaw to satisfy the essential needs of all the city's inhabitants. Determination still burned to complete these dreams. The Polish government had made Warsaw its capital in February this year. Warsaw wallowed in near-death throes five months earlier, but she did not succumb. Now no time was wasted in setting up the Warsaw Reconstruction Office.

Stefan's heart swelled with pride as he thought, *Warsaw lives again. And perhaps his Uncle Jósef has had a small part in it. He knew his uncle's heart had never left his homeland.*

He parked the car in front of the building that temporarily housed the office of The Ministry of Art and Culture. Frederic had all the necessary paperwork, and he was waiting for him in the director's office.

"Count Zurowski," Director Bosko stood and extended his hand in greeting, "so honored to have you here. And what your steward has laid out for me is beyond believable."

Stefan acknowledged the greeting and walked to the table that held the pictures. Uncle Jósef had obtained a prototype of a camera that took pictures in color using a special film.

The pictures that Frederic had taken and developed were laid out on a long table in front of the director's desk. There was one picture each, depicting the various village shops doing business on the Zurowski estate. Frederic had captured the workers at their trades. Pastoral scenes caught the cattle on verdant pastures, grazing contentedly on the lush grass.

Ish Jacobson's artistry in the castle courtyard and gardens was on display, water fountains throwing sprays colored with the spectrum of the rainbow. The art of topiary was evident in the privet hedges. Flower beds were stunning in the choice of placement and hue.

The twelve statues to the entrance of the castle were undamaged even though they'd marched there since the Middle Ages. Bas-reliefs in limestone against the red brick walls were pictured: Christ at the well with the Samaritan woman; Christ praying in the Garden of Gethsemane; the Last Supper. Pictures of the tall, arched windows, throwing shadows on the tile floors, and scenes that were painted long ago above interior entranceways Frederic had painstakingly caught the vaulted ceilings, the flying buttresses, the very essence of the Gothic Edifice.

But it was inside the castle that the heritage was most evident. Bedchambers with furnishings that bespoke of the time period. Kitchens that had served many past generations. It was all there.

"Ah, Frederic, these are indeed masterpieces," Stefan said.

"Indeed, yes," Mr. Bosko added. "The Zurowski Estate with its villages will be the main feature for a tourist excursion. These pictures will make beautiful souvenirs. Our own citizens will be encouraged to see such restoration on your estate. And we're hearing of many travelers from abroad who are planning a visit already."

"The village shops are, as of now, self-sustaining. The families living in the cottages will be allowed to stay and their children will be allowed to inherit," said Stefan. "A trust has been established for the maintenance and upkeep of the estate; Frederic and Ish Jacobson, along with those they appoint, will set dates and times for such visits," Stefan emphasized. "I think it's all spelled out in the agreement."

"Yes. Frederic went over the details very carefully with our entire staff," Bosko nodded his head.

"One thing I've come to add," Stefan began, "is that the Zurowski Jeweled Crucifix will be displayed in a securely-made case with the latest electronic protection for all who visit."

"The Crucifix?" stammered Bosko, sitting down hard in his chair. "I thought that was merely legend." He paused, then asked, "it really exists?"

'It has been in the Zurowski family for generations. Frederic has prepared a written history of where it originated and when and how we obtained it." Stefan took the last picture that Frederic handed him from his briefcase.

"This piece will require a brochure all its own," Bosko touched the picture, reverently.

"We will, of course, prepare the display case ourselves," Stefan said.

"Of course," Bosko agreed. "You know," he went on, "many years ago we tried to get your father to open the castle for visitors, but he denied us. It's so much like the Malbork Castle, even the same builder."

"This is a new day. This is the time to let the history of Poland be known and appreciated. My Uncle Józef Zurowski and I want to help this happen."

"Józef Zurowski. Now that's a name that is revered throughout the city. The provisions that he was able to channel into the Ghetto and into all of the city are indeed legendary."

"Frederic," began Stefan, "is there anything more I need to do?"

"Sign this one agreement, then all is in order," Frederic slid the page across the table.

"Gentlemen, I really don't know what to say. This is a milestone in perpetuating Poland's rich history and its love for the land," Bosko stood, offering his hand as they prepared to leave.

After the two men left, Bosko sat looking at the picture of the crucifix for a long time, crossed himself, gathered up the rest of the pictures, and locked them in the wall safe behind his desk.

Beads of rain sparkled like diamonds on the hood of the Rolls as they drove back to the home of the jeweler. Satisfaction settled on each face.

"It will be too hot an item to steal, Frederic, with all of Poland watching," a chuckle of relief escaped him. "If the belief of good fortune holds, no one will want to risk Poland's future."

"I think this is a wise plan, Stefan. One worthy and reminiscent of your father," Frederic added.

Their laughter mingled and echoed throughout the car.

"The Warsaw Reconstruction Office reports that before winter 500 pre-fabricated houses, one and two rooms, were built in Warsaw," said David Jacobson.

David Jacobson had joined them at the jeweler's house and Stefan, Ish Jacobson, Jack, and Mr. Wócjąk's sat around the table listening to the news that David had learned at his meeting with the group at that office.

"That'll be a blessing to the ones who get to move in these houses, but it won't be nearly enough," said Frederic.

"It's a 'gift' from Germany," sneered David, "and I don't know how I feel about that."

"Ah, David, you've seen too much," his brother sympathized, "it'll keep many off the streets, and the houses will have water and lights."

"What other improvements are to be seen soon?" asked Stefan.

"The electricity plant is being repaired, and the water supply plant repairs are underway," answered David. "Work is being done on broadcasting stations, telephone installations, streetlights, streetcars, and a new bridge over the Vistula should be completed by the middle of next year."

"So much, so quickly," exclaimed Stefan.

"Our people believe in the worth of reconstruction, their love for the city, and with enthusiasm, they gladly sacrifice to make these things possible," Mr. Wócjąk's face glowed with the fervor of his speech.

David raised his fist in the air and declared, "Warsaw lives again!"

Chapter 36

Frederic was up early to help Mr. Wócjąk get the food on the table before the men came to breakfast. Outside, light was just beginning to shoulder through the clouds. Somewhere a rooster hailed its coming.

"I'm gonna hate to see all of you leave," Mr. Wócjąk looked around.

"You won't be glad to have your house back to yourself?" asked Ish, patting the older man's arm.

"Oh, no," he said quickly, "offering shelter to you all has given me purpose. I'm coming back to life. I no longer focus on the devastation outside my windows. My bed is still empty and no one sits across from me at my table, but I'm healing."

"Stefan would gladly offer you a place to set up your jewelry shop in the village on the Zurowski Estate," Ish offered.

"Would Count Zurowski really do that?" the old man's voice trembled. "I wouldn't need much space."

"I'm sure he would consider it an honor to have an artisan such as yourself setting up shop in the village."

"My clients would consider it desirable to come to the estate of Count Zurowski to visit my shop. The old Count never encouraged visitors," he paused, then rushed on. "I'm not saying anything against the old Count."

"It's alright. Stefan likes to say, 'it's a new day'," Ish brushed aside Mr. Wócjąk's embarrassment.

Stefan, David, Frederic, and Jack entered the room and quickly settled at the table. As Grace was said before eating, a prayer for the safety of the men was added.

"So, you won't be coming along with us back to Domani z Camin?" Stefan looked at Ish.

"No, David and I will come as soon as we make the trip to the liberated extermination camps," Ish answered.

"Yes, I need to document the unspeakable conditions the liberators confronted. This should help shed light on the full scope of Nazi horrors. My diaries are eyewitness accounts of inhumane conditions and atrocities in the Warsaw Ghetto, and these final pages will show where those Jews that were rounded up were taken. The numbers are staggering," David paused, "we may never know exactly."

"Auschwitz was liberated in January of this year," said Frederic. "Have you been there?"

"No, I was injured in Warsaw before I could make that trip," said David. "Ish found me here and saved my life."

"Maybe, just saved your leg," Ish brushed off the compliment. Laughter eased the tension.

"Yeah, guess that's right," chuckled David. "Anyway, the Americans liberated Buchenwald, Dora-Mittelbau, Flossenburg, Dachau, and Mauthausen."

"I read where the British forces liberated the camps in northern Germany, including Neuengamme and Bergen-Belsen," interrupted Jack.

"I'm sketching pictures," David continued, "so what I draw will complete my recorded documents. I'm scheduled to have them in Nuremberg in July. The trials start in August."

"I've seen your 'sketching'," scoffed Frederic. "Your drawings are perfection."

David just bowed his head.

"It's only fitting that the trials be held at Nuremberg," added Stefan, "since that was the birthplace of Naziism."

"It was a cold-hearted slut that gave birth to that brain-child," sneered David. "I'm glad the trials are starting in August. Can't be too soon for me."

"Stefan, Mr. Wócjąk has expressed an interest in relocating his shop to the village on Zurowski land," Ish eased to another subject.

"We'd be honored," Stefan agreed. "Let it be soon."

"I'd be pleased if you could be there for my wedding," said Jack. "In case everyone has forgotten, Monica expects me back on time."

Laughter filled the small kitchen, shifting attention off of David.

"I wouldn't wanna face Monica's wrath," Stefan winked at Jack. "Does she know yet that your sister is coming from Scotland to check her out? See if she's suitable for a laird's wife?"

Jack groaned, shaking his head. *I wonder what Monica meant when she said she needed to talk to me before the ceremony. I hadn't had time to tell her about the unexpected visit yet.*

"Lookin' forward to that meeting," continued Stefan.

"Deliver us from older sisters!" Jack threw up his hands in surrender.

"We may hear that explosion all the way to where we'll be," Ish couldn't stop his teasing.

"Well, you'd just better be back in time for the wedding, or Monica may display more fireworks," Stefan told Ish.

"We'll be there for sure. David and I both will need time for decompression after we visit the death camps," Ish stood. "David, let's get started."

David and Ish headed west driving the Nazi touring car that David had stripped and refurbished. Poetic justice was on the road for all to see.

Stefan, Frederic, and Jack headed northeast toward the Zurowski land where there would be village festivities, celebrating the wedding of Jack and Monica. The stuff of life, proving that 'there is time for every activity under the heavens: a time to be born and a time to die, a time to plant and a time to uproot, a time to kill and a time to heal,'…

Chapter 37

The return to Domani z Camin was like being bathed with warm oil. Peace flowed, lessening the horror of the scenes they'd left in Warsaw. Still, many signs that pointed to new growth in the city, poking like spring flowers through an icy crust.

The opportunity was too good to ignore. The upcoming wedding had triggered this awakening, but the entire village was now alive with a need to celebrate. The demand to come out from under the clouds of war burst forth in a spirit of jubilee; each house was freshly painted, and an abundance of flowers crowded the window boxes. Polish flags waved above every shop along with the banner advertising the wares that could be found within. Windowpanes winked back at the metal windchimes hanging from trees where the winds treated them gently. The children's maypoles were left up for the festivities.

"I don't know what to say," Stefan's voice choked at the sight of the village. "Frederic, have you ever seen the village like this?"

The men exited the car and were in awe of the view they were seeing.

"Stefan, long ago before you were born," Frederic paused to wipe his eyes, "when your mother was alive, we had many festivals."

"Ah dinnae ken," exclaimed Jack, "I guess I'll have to get married now. Looks like the whole village has started the party already."

The Knight's Hall filled with laughter as they all gathered early for the evening meal so that Konrad and Jan could be part of the occasion.

Stefan looked around at those at the table. Many stories were evident here. Each person had come to Poland, interacted with others, and no one would remain the same. Some would return with him, some would stay here, but each one would be forever changed.

The smaller gathering room beside the Knight's Hall was again their destination after eating, and the talk was quiet. Konrad and Jan were beginning to yawn and lay their heads on their daddy's chest.

"Momma," Stefan whispered to Sophia, "time to put these boys to bed." Sophia led the way as Stefan followed with both boys in his arms.

One by one each sought their rooms, weary after the long day, leaving Monica and Jack alone.

"Miss me?" Jack pulled Monica onto his lap.

She stood suddenly and walked over by the window looking out into the starlit night.

"Monica, what's wrong?'" He followed her.

"It's me," her voice was husky.

"What about you?" he asked. He held her against him, her back resting against his chest.

"Do you remember what I told you about my brother, Maurice, being," she paused for breath, "sexually 'different'?"

"I remember. You said you thought Stefan blamed you for not knowing about Maurice's treatment of Sophia and telling someone. You don't still think that do you?"

"No. What if it affected me?"

"From what you've told me, it affected everyone. Just in different ways. Your grandmother felt guilty for not watching out for you properly, Sophia and Stefan's marriage got off to," he paused, "a rocky start."

"True, but…" Sophia interrupted.

"Your Uncle Jósef was deceived. Maurice's work for your uncle was above reproach, and he had no reason to suspect the abuse that Sophia suffered from Maurice for so many years."

"I know, but…" Sophia tried again to interrupt.

"Even Maurice couldn't face being found out and ran," finished Jack.

"What if I am obsessed with you?" Monica's face flushed as she blurted out her fear.

He turned her in his arms and rested his forehead against her own. "Obsess over me all you want. I think I can take it."

"Jack, I'm serious. All the time you were gone, I couldn't think of anything else—only wanted you to come back. My mind was filled with you!"

"I love you, too, Monica," he whispered against her lips before capturing her mouth with his.

Monica slipped her arms around his neck, and Jack held her tightly against him.

"Love?" asks Monica. "Is this what I'm feeling? It kinda hurts when you're away." She lifted her face to be kissed again.

"Monica, how did I get so lucky. My tough, aloof, green-eyed beauty is going to be putty in my hands."

"Don't be so sure; some of my thoughts about you aren't so pure," she retorted.

"Oh, Monica, I think I'll be able to withstand that, too," he laughed, pulling her against him again.

"Jack, seriously," Monica started, "I know you were married before and lost your wife. Maybe, I won't be able to measure up to her."

"Monica, I was incredibly young and was told, as the future laird, I should marry to keep our line going. I thought I loved Alice, but what we had didn't last. She only wanted a child and when our son was born, I was no longer in her world.

"May I ask how she and your son died?" Monica ask hesitantly.

"Of course. Monica, I'll never keep anything from you." He stared overhead as in thought. "It looked like a storm was brewing, but she was determined that she and our son have their afternoon ride. I asked her not to ride too far or go near the cliffs. I was expecting buyers and couldn't go with them.

"Anyway, when they were found, it looked as if their horses had spooked and thrown them both. Alice was dead, and little Jack lived for only a few hours. He was three, the age of Konrad. He was able to tell me that lightning had scared him. When the horses were found, they had been electrocuted when the lightning struck their metal shoes. Funny, it never did rain."

"Oh, Jack, I'm so sorry. I didn't know."

"It was hard. His little body was so broken, but I was able to hold him as he died."

"How could you forgive her?" Monica was angry.

"Forgiveness didn't come easy," Jack answered. "God had to help, and I knew Alice loved little Jack too much to ever deliberately hurt him.

"I've found further consolation in trying to carry on my father's work until a pastor could be found. I only taught bible studies that I had learned from him, but I've always had a love for God in my heart."

They sat on the sofa together, relaxing in each other's presence.

"Oh, Jack, we're going to have a wonderful life together," Monica's sigh was deep.

"Ah dinnae ken, lass," he paused, a smile twitching the corners of his mouth, "do you think you will continue to have those 'not-so-pure' thoughts about me?"

"Laddie, if you don't move your hand from where it's resting right now, I can guarantee it."

"Caught me," Jack laughed, as he moved his hand behind her neck to pull her in for one last good-night kiss.

Chapter 38

It was predawn and Ish lay beside Manka drawing strength from her closeness. She was his touchstone and the one person in the world that he could pour out his heart to.

"I have nothing more to give him, Manka," Ish whispered. "David isn't the younger brother that I knew. It's as though he emptied all that was 'David' fighting with the Resistance in the Warsaw Ghetto, and he now identifies with those who are appointed to bring the war criminals to justice."

"He still plans to take his diaries to Nuremberg, doesn't he?" asked Manka. "You said they were detailed, and he'd added sketches.

"Yes, but more than that, he plans to stay until the entire trial is over. He's determined to push his own agenda."

"And what's that?"

"Complete exposure of the forced labor programs, the ghetto life of the Jews, and the degradation of Poles, causing the death of so many. He's lost the ability to focus on anything else. Even his daughter."

"I'm sure he's glad for her safety," Manka protested.

"Sure, but he feels guilty that he couldn't save her at Jedwabne, and I think that's where his hardness started," Ish said. "I think Leah understands this, but it's hurt her."

"Leah has Stan, and soon they'll be with his family in America," Manka offered.

Legacy Redeemed

"Thank God for that," Ish said. "I have to let David go; I have nothing more of myself to give."

"You've done enough, Ish. You found him, saved his life, and let him know his family is safe."

"Maybe sometime in the future, when his scars from this war are healing, he'll regain his ability to love."

"We'll be patient, and we'll be here at Domani z Camin for him when he comes to himself."

"Manka, you're so good for me," Ish snuggled closer to his wife. "What would I do without you?"

"I'll never let you find out," her laughter was muffled in his chest.

Nature came rejoicing in June with an abundance of growth in the fields, gardens, and high spirits of those living in the village and the castle on the newly-restored Zurowski lands. It was all as before, only better. Stefan, as the new Count, extended an essence of welcome that had been missing when his father ruled. The land wasn't his; he was the caretaker. Now, his legacy is redeemed, a new legacy in his ability to care for it and for those living within its boundaries.

The wedding was a week away and the trip to Danzig to board the *Baltic Queen* would follow two weeks after that. There was a whirlwind of activity that caught up everyone on the estate. Ish and Jack were putting the finishing touches on the wooden arch that the bride and groom would stand under for the ceremony, but Ish would cover it with fresh flowers from the castle gardens the night before.

The kitchens were staffed with extra help from the village under the close scrutiny of Kasia and Manka. Every dish that had ever conceivably graced a table for a wedding feast was being prepared. The tantalizing odors escaped the kitchens to find their way into the Knight's Hall and the after-dinner gathering room. If the diners were disappointed that their evening suppers didn't live up to the aromas in the air, they didn't dare say so.

Monica was putting final adjustments on her wedding gown, Sophia's matron-of-honor dress was finished, and they both helped Leah finish her bridesmaid dress. Konrad boasted that he was the ring bearer, and Aunt Monkey couldn't get married without him.

First, it was just a speck that Stefan noticed in the sky, but soon he recognized it to be a plane. The last planeload of supplies from America had landed a couple of days ago and had just left this morning. This plane had a flag of Scotland, a white saltire interfacing a blue field. It was the correct flag for all private individuals and corporate bodies to fly.

As Stefan watched the plane come in for the landing, Jack drove up beside him in the Rolls.

"Your sister?" asked Stefan.

"'fraid so," Jack laughed, "and I haven't told Monica yet."

"Does your sister not fly the Union Jack?" Stefan teased.

"It's on the other side of the plane," Jack answered, "but it is smaller. One of the Scots who didn't surrender. Get in, and we'll meet her together."

They rode together toward the plane as it taxied to the hangar.

"My older sister might be the reincarnation of Lady Christian Bruce who fought actively in the war against the English," his words were spoken fondly. "Now her fighting spirit keeps our business flourishing and all the crofters in line."

"Crofters?" asked Stefan.

"Yes, you can compare them to the tenant farmers that you have on your land," Jack explained.

Jack embraced his sister and introduced her and the pilot to Stefan. The pilot was toting a pet carrier.

"So, where's the bride-to-be?" Christina asked, bluntly. "I've brought her dog."

"Her dog?" Stefan's eyebrow lifted.

"All new MacKenzie brides are presented with a Skye Terrier as a welcome into the family."

"Christina, that tradition might have waited until we arrived home," Jack chuckled.

"Tradition is tradition. She'll get her dog."

They all four settled in the Rolls and started back toward the castle.

"I haven't told her you were coming," Jack admitted. "It'll be a surprise."

"Guess you're protecting the shy little thing," Christina laughed.

"Not exactly;" said Jack, "maybe I'm protecting you!"

"Really?" she quirked her eyebrow. "I'm as big as you, Jack."

Christina did stand as tall as Jack with shoulders that filled out her tweed jacket. She had an hourglass figure, except the sand clock was of sturdy proportions. But the term 'handsome' would describe the lady with light eyes the color of Jack's and close-cropped gold hair that sparked red.

"Bruce didn't want to come with you?" Jack asked after his younger brother.

"Nay, the lad said he couldn't leave his sheep that long," said Christina.

The trip from the airstrip to the castle was a short one, and those inside the castle had come to the front entrance at the sound of the plane.

Stefan stood beside Sophia, "This is the Countess, my wife."

"Just Sophia, please," Sophia blushed.

"Ah, yes, Countess Sophia," Christina offered her hand. "And the lass behind you must be Jack's intended?"

Leah stepped forward, extending her hand. "No, madam, I'm Leah Janda."

Stefan stepped forward and continued the introductions.

"So," Christina raised her voice, "is the bride-to-be in hiding?"

"Not in the least," Monica called out gayly as she hurried out the door to join the others. She went to Jack, linking her arm with his. "You must be my future sister-in-law," she paused, "Jack, why didn't you tell me she was coming?"

"I hadn't had a chance, lass," Jack hedged.

"We're very glad you could make it for our wedding." Jack didn't flinch, but he would have a bruise where Monica pinched his arm.

With the aplomb of a duchess, Monica took over the awkward situation. "Come with me. I'll show you the wedding dress I designed." Linking arms with the confused Christina, she swept her into the castle away from the others.

Christina took the pet carrier from the pilot, "Yes, I need to see if it's appropriate. And I have the MacKenzie bride gift for you."

Stefan and Jack watched the two women leave the room, and they could only guess at how the conversation would go.

No cloud dared mar the sky on the day of the wedding. The wind blew only a warm, gentle breeze, keeping the temperature at a perfect number.

The ślub held in the church was attended only by the residents of the castle along with the bridal attendants. As the music began, Monica took Stefan's arm and they began down the aisle.

Stefan bowed his head and whispered, "You've done well, Monica. Jack can't take his eyes off you." Monica blushed, adding a glow that's only seen on a bride's face on her wedding day.

As per the Polish tradition, Jack hadn't seen his bride in her wedding gown until she walked toward him down the aisle of the village church. She was a vision of loveliness that even the cameras wouldn't be able to capture.

Stefan released his hold on Monica's arm as the question of giving the bride away needed to be answered. He put her hand into Jack's hand.

Konrad's brow furrowed in concentration, waiting for the time he was to offer the rings resting on the satin pillow he carried. He relaxed when he no longer had to balance the pillow, and he let out an audible sigh of relief, causing a whisper of laughter from the congregation.

The ceremony was complete. The bride and groom led the way out of the church where the crowd was ready to start the wedding party in the Knight's Hall. The overflow from the Hall would be seated in the courtyard on long benches on either side of long tables, allowing for most of those attending to be seated. Some youngsters brought blankets where they could picnic on the grass under the trees.

The women of the village added their culinary masterpieces to the already heavily-laden tables. The children arrived dressed as characters of the stories told by their 'story book' lady. The men stood back, smiling as though they had orchestrated the entire event.

The band was at the entrance of the castle near to the courtyard. There was room for dancing in the Knight's Hall, and an outside bandstand had been constructed close enough to the Hall so the music could spill out to all who wanted to dance. The merriment at the party was heightened by the fact that the war was over. Life could return to normal; it would be a new normal, but the fear of losing more family members in battle was put to rest.

Fireflies signaled the beginning of dusk, and food was no longer replenished on the tables. Dishes, leftovers, and tablecloths were taken to the kitchens. Tomorrow would be the second wedding party, the poprawiny. Another all-day party celebrating the best day of the newlywed couple's life all over again.

"Monica?" Jack stood close to Monica so his words would be heard only by her. "What is this second-day party?"

"A Polish custom of repeating the marriage all over again," explained Monica. "Also, it's a way to eat all the other food that's been prepared. And more dancing."

"Is the first one legal?" Jack ask, smiling.

"Of course," Monica said.

"Would they miss us if we skipped the second party?" Jack winked.

"I thought you'd never ask," Monica's smile told him all he needed to know.

"Christina's plane is already taking her home," Jack said. "And you do know that there's to be another ceremony when we get to Scotland, don't you?"

"Yes, she mentioned it," Monica's tone was merry, "and I told her if you tied the knot with me twice, you'd never get away."

"Well, there is that, too. But we have to have bagpipes with marching and all the crofters in attendance. The marriage of their laird isn't legal if it isn't done at home."

"I don't know if you're serious or not, but I told Christina I'd have to have another bridal gown. Mine can only be worn once. It will be packed away here," Monica said.

"Certainly is tough blending two countries," Jack added.

"Try three. I'm American, so maybe having Konrad as ring bearer and tossing my wedding bouquet counted for that."

"I love your wedding gown, but how long will it take you to change?" asked Jack. "My suitcase is in the Rolls already."

"You didn't think I might want to attend another party tomorrow in my honor?" teased Monica.

"I was just hoping, lass," he said.

"My wardrobe here is limited, so it won't take long to pack. I see major shopping in my near future."

Jack turned her and gently push her forward. "Go, then. Slip away when you can and meet me where the bridge leads from the castle."

Jack watched her go for a minute, then turned from the castle.

"Maybe things can return to normal." It was David who was walking toward Jack from the shadows. "I'm dedicating myself to making it happen." Lack of sunlight emphasized the deep lines in David's face, the moonlight turned his white hair silver.

"I think the 'Fantasy Mist' in the Warsaw Ghetto has already been a champion of the victims," Jack said to David.

David chuckled. "Sounds much too heroic. I just did what I could, and I was fortunate enough to survive unlike so many working at my side."

"I know Leah was glad to see you," said Jack.

"Ah, yes, my little girl," David sighed. "When the trials in Nuremberg are over, I plan to visit her in America. But I'll live here at Domani z Camin until my heart thaws a little. I owe that to Ish."

The two men stood in silence, each in his own thoughts.

"Guess I'd better tell someone where we're going. We're driving to Krakow, and then I want to drive through the town of Gryfino to show Monica The Crooked Forest on our way back to meet everyone in Warsaw."

"Good plan. Krakow is one of the few places that hasn't been damaged, and it's a beautiful, old town. The pine trees in The Crooked Forest are a sight to see; they look like giant letter 'J's', growing from the base, then taking a sharp 90-degree turn back up."

"Well, this honeymoon will do until places in Europe are again available to tourists. I'm sure I don't care where we go, but brides seem to want to go to Paris," Jack's tone was light.

"Best of luck in your marriage," David extended his hand. "I'll make sure your new bride makes it safely after dark to the bridge. I saw where you hid your car."

The men's laughter floated in the night as they went their separate ways.

Chapter 39

Stefan stayed at Domani z Camin long enough to see that everything was in order after the pąprawiny. The second party had lasted throughout the day and way up into the night. No one let the absence of the bride and groom dampen their festivities for long. Now a week later all signs of revelry were gone. Everyone had returned to the care of the land and their shops, lighter in their steps and their outlooks for the future. Revival had come to this little piece of Poland.

David Jacobson would be driving them to Warsaw where Monica and Jack would be waiting for them. It would be a tight trip from Warsaw to Danzig to meet the *Baltic Queen*. The estate car Stefan ordered for Ish hadn't been delivered yet.

Leah, Stanislas, little Noelle, and Sarah would ride with David in his stripped-down Nazi touring car on to Danzig, while Jack would drive the Rolls back with Monica, Stefan, Sophia, Konrad, and Jan. They'd made room in David's larger car for the provisions that Manka and Kasia had packed for the journey, and room was made for baby Noelle's necessities.

Captain Joyce had assured Stefan that everything they'd left on the *Baltic Queen* two years ago was still packed in their quarters just as they'd left it. They would only need clothes for their journey to the ship but nothing more. Sophia assured the boys that there were toys on board the ship, but Konrad had put all his Lego blocks in a bag and Jan carried his bear.

Mr. Wócjąk, now permanently settled at Domani z Camin, had loaned his house in Warsaw for the use of those traveling. When David returned from Danzig to Warsaw, he would use it for his headquarters while gathering more background material before he and his associates headed for the Nuremberg trials.

Stan and Leah were able to adopt the orphaned Sarah. They'd grown very fond of the girl, and she'd panicked at the thought of being left behind. Everyone loved the quiet, unassuming child that had seen too much evil, but healing had taken place as she became a playmate to Konrad and Jan. Now she was officially a big sister to baby Noelle.

The trip from the Zurowski estate to Warsaw was tiring, and they were all glad to arrive at Mr. Wócjąk's house where they could recover. After supper, they were ready to turn in and get an early start the next day.

Morning found them again squeezed into their automobiles headed to Danzig. The roads were cleared of much of the rubble, and the smoother roads allowed for a faster speed. The people of Warsaw were wasting no time bringing order from the chaos. Shops along the cleared roads were opening once again.

They stopped at a brightly-lit bakery to buy rolls and fresh coffee from a jolly proprietor who welcomed them with a renewed sense of hope for the future. He sent them off with a smile and a loaf of bread for their trip to Danzig.

There she stood, outlined by a brilliant, setting sun. Stefan thought the *Baltic Queen* had never looked so welcoming. He led the way up the gangplank where Captain Joyce greeted them all.

"Mister Brown," he indicated a waiting crewman, "will show you all to your quarters. Dinner will be in two hours, so you'll have time to unwind and freshen up."

Stefan and Captain Joyce watched them leave the deck to follow the crew member. Stefan could tell that Captain Joyce had something more to say.

"A communique came an hour ago for you," said the Captain. "I've printed a copy for you to read." The lines on the Captain's face deepened as he handed the paper to Stefan. His eyes were bright with unshed tears.

Chapter 40

Stefan still held the letter in his hand. He didn't remember when he had crushed its pages, but he was still clutching them to his chest when Sophia came into the room. She didn't speak, but she came up to him, wrapping her arms around his waist and laying her head on his chest.

She was ever in-tuned to him. Since their first time together, she had been his soulmate. His father, the Count, may have arranged for their marriage, but she had always been destined for him. A blessing in store from his Heavenly Father. He had never looked at another. She had given him two sons, a legacy to carry the story of past Zurowskis into the future.

The boys had flourished here in his native land. The first-born son was always given the name Konrad. Not only did their five-year-old son carry the name, but his features were a daily reminder to Stefan of the older brother he'd lost. Jan was three now and like his mother had hair the color of the sun and a feisty spirit to match. No difference would be made between the boys. The legacy belonged to both of them; the responsibility was enough to be shared.

"Stefan, my love, what's wrong?" Sofia now raised her face to look into his eyes.

"This letter," he said. He turned his eyes stared at a place over her shoulder.

"Yes?"

"Uncle Jósef is gone," he said. His cheeks were wet with tears.

"When my mother married him, he became a father to me," said Sofia, her voice choked.

"Yes, more of a father than my father was to me."

"What happened?" asked Sophia.

"Seems his heart gave out. Your mother writes that it was quite sudden, and he went without pain," Stefan said. "He had kept his condition from us when we left to come here. I'm afraid that I left him with too much responsibility. But it was our dream, his and mine, for me to return and restore Domani z Camin."

"You can't take on any blame. You did for him what he couldn't do for himself," said Sophia. "He would be proud of the restoration of the estate. It's again self-sustaining, workers now have a future. Poland has a new memorial."

"Their priest held a private graveside service. Remember, there was a plot of land near Forest House dedicated for use as a Zurowski family cemetery when Maurice died? Uncle Jósef was buried there. Marie says there will be a memorial service at the church with the entire town attending when we return," he said.

"We are going home!" Sofia said. She clutched his arm, tightly.

"Yes, little Sophia, home," he answered. "But our route will remain the same. We will go to Scotland first, as planned, to leave Jack and Monica, and Jack's car is loaded on the *Baltic Queen*.

"Oh, Stefan, I've loved every minute here with all the restoration, but it is now done, and my heart longs for home," she said. "Konrad will need to start school this fall," she paused, "and I want our next child to be born at Forest House."

"Our next child?" he questioned. He held Sophia away from him and looked into her shining eyes. "Really?"

"Happy?' she asked.

"Sophia, this is life. A generation passes, and there must be those to take its place. Let's fill Forest House with Zurowskis!" he shouted.

"It certainly seems we've been trying!" Sophia laughed. "Stefan, Jósef would have loved for children's laughter to fill Forest House. He longed for children of his own."

"We'll talk of Uncle Jósef on our way home; we will grieve, but we can have our own memorial."

Captain Joyce had refitted the sleeping quarters to make the trip back even more comfortable. The cargo that had come over on the *Queen* was offloaded, making its way on to Domani z Camin. Konrad and Jan bounced up and down at this new adventure.

The boys and Sarah had a new playmate with Monica's little Skye Terrier. Its hair was so light gray that in the sun it silvered, contrasting with the black outline on its head. It would lessen the boredom for the children of the nearly month-long trip on the ship. Fortunately, Christina had completed the potty-on-the-paper training before bringing the new puppy to Monica.

They sailed the North Sea, blue waters blending with the blue of the sky when they reached the Port of Cromarty Firth. Jack's sister, younger brother, and all the crofters living on MacKenzie land were there to meet them at the dock.

"They're glad to see you home," Stefan clapped Jack on the back.

"No doubt Christina has the wedding all planned," Jack shook his head. "But Monica told me that she'd planned the first wedding, and this one will just be like a stage play, so she'd let Christina direct it. Monica thought that might soften the blow when Christina learns that the bride-gift terrier will live in America with the boys." The men's laughter joined.

They all watched as Monica stooped and said goodbye to the boys. Konrad was sniffling softly, but he ran his hands over the puppy's back, and he shook his head in agreement with what Monica was saying to him.

The Rolls Royce was off-loaded and they all waved until the car was out of sight. Jack had assured Stefan that he and Monica would be at Forest House to attend Uncle Jósef's memorial service. And while there, he would research the possibility of opening a branch store from their New York retail facility in Dark Forest that would necessitate future business trips. He considered them all family.

Stefan and Sophia and those sailing back home with them were content with their decisions. Their task was done. Domani z Camin was once again flourishing, and it was left in the caring hands of people who loved the land. The castle and lands would become a Polish National Treasure open for visitors from far and wide, under the watchful eye of a Zurowski Crucifix encased in the Knight's Hall for all to see.

The memorial service for Jósef would signal the end of the first Zurowski generation in America, but the second generation would be encircled by memories from the past and plans for the future. The town traditions would carry on.

Stefan now shouldered leadership of the Zurowski empire. There would be much change in industry at the war's end, but Jósef had left talented leadership in place who could continue under the authority of his nephew. Jósef had prepared Stefan well.

Epilogue

Three months later...

Supper was over, and the boys were asleep. The staff had finished for the night, and the house was quiet. Stefan and Sophia were finally alone in their suite, snuggling together on a soft sofa.

"Stefan, do you think the crucifix will be safe? Do you think leaving it there will compromise the good fortune associated with Zurowski possession? No family member remains at Domani z Camin now."

"The *genuine* crucifix is with the Zurowski family," Stefan answered.

"But…oh, I see," Sophia sighed. "I should have known. So, all is good."

"All is good," pronounced Stefan. "And how are you, my love?"

"So, content." Her belly rose with her sigh.

"And what shall we name our next son?" he asked. He gently put his hand on her protruding belly.

"Anne Marie," Sophia answered with a smile.

www.ingramcontent.com/pod-product-compliance
Lightning Source LLC
LaVergne TN
LVHW011935070526
838202LV00054B/4650